THE SCOOP
— & —
BEHIND THE SCREEN

AGATHA CHRISTIE, DOROTHY L. SAYERS,
HUGH WALPOLE, E. C. BENTLEY,
ANTHONY BERKELEY, CLEMENCE DANE,
RONALD KNOX, AND FREEMAN WILLS CROFTS
Introduction by Julian Symons

BERKLEY BOOKS, NEW YORK

"The Scoop" first appeared as a serial in *The Listener* in 1931.
"Behind the Screen" first appeared as a serial in *The Listener* in 1930

The Publishers are indebted to the Dorothy L. Sayers Historical
and Literary Society for the text of the original serial extracts
from *The Listener*. They have endeavored to trace the copyright
holders of the appendixes to this book, but without success.

This Berkley book contains the complete
text of the original hardcover edition.
It has been completely reset in a typeface
designed for easy reading and was printed
from new film.

THE SCOOP & BEHIND THE SCREEN

A Berkley Book / published by arrangement with Harper & Row,
Publishers, Inc., as "A Cornelia & Michael Bessie Book"

PRINTING HISTORY
Harper & Row edition published 1983
Charter edition / December 1984
Berkley edition / May 1986

ISBN: 0-425-09696-3

A BERKLEY BOOK ® TM 757,375
Berkley Books are published by The Berkley Publishing Group,
200 Madison Avenue, New York, NY 10016.
The name "Berkley" and the "B" logo
are trademarks belonging to Berkley Publishing Corporation.

PRINTED IN THE UNITED STATES OF AMERICA

10   9   8   7   6   5   4   3   2

Great Names in Mystery

CONTENTS

THE SCOOP
&
BEHIND THE SCREEN

PREFACE: A BRIEF ACCOUNT OF THE DETECTION CLUB

"The Detection Club was founded in 1932"—those were the opening words of an introduction I wrote a few years ago for a collection of stories by the club's members, *Verdict of Thirteen*. The present book shows that they were mistaken, for these two broadcast serials went on the air in 1930 and 1931. How did the mistake arise, what is the truth? And indeed, you may ask if you have picked up this volume casually, what is the Detection Club?

It is a slew (surely the right collective noun) of crime writers, numbering at the club's foundation twenty-six, and at present roughly twice that number. The original members all wrote stories of pure detection, "it being understood that the term 'detective-novel' does not include adventure-stories or 'thrillers' or stories in which the detection is not a main interest." In the changed climate of today this rule has been relaxed, and the club members now include writers of racing thrillers like Dick Francis, adventure stories like Geoffrey Household, spy stories like Len Deighton. The original members, apart from the contributors to this book, included such celebrated writers of the period as H. C. Bailey, G. D. H. Cole, J. J. Connington, R. Austin Freeman, A. E. W. Mason, A. A. Milne, Baroness Orczy and John Rhode. It may be remarked that all these were British writers, and only two Americans have been members of the club, John Dickson Carr and Patricia Highsmith. Chauvinism is not responsible for this British preponderance. Membership is by invitation, and since the club was from the beginning and has remained essentially a dining club, there seemed no point in electing members who would be very unlikely to eat our dinners. Americans living in Britain, as Carr and Highsmith did for some years, were welcomed.

And when *was* the club founded? We have no papers of any kind relating to meetings before the fifties—their whereabouts, if they exist, is a mystery none of the present members has been able to solve, and all the original members are dead. We do possess a little book of Constitution and Rules dated 1932, and wrongly assumed that to have been the foundation year. When we learned our mistake, a serious attempt was made to find the true date, a magnum of champagne being offered to the first person who could give factual information fixing a date, in the form, perhaps, of a menu card which said: "First dinner of the Detection Club, held on . . ."

Perhaps it was too much to hope for a menu card. Certainly none appeared. A Brighton bookseller, however, won the magnum by sending details of a letter written to the *Times Literary Supplement* in 1930, signed by several members of the Detection Club. But was 1930 the true date? One member, Anthony Berkeley, claimed to have founded the club in 1928, and there may have been informal meetings in that year, but until some cache of priceless documents is revealed, we are prepared to settle for 1930.

The present volume, the contents of which have never been reprinted since they appeared in the BBC's weekly periodical *The Listener*, was written to provide funds so that club premises might be acquired. Other books with the same purpose, also the product of several hands, were *The Floating Admiral* (1931), which has recently been reprinted; *Ask a Policeman* (1933), soon to reappear; and of course the recent *Verdict of Thirteen*, already mentioned. There are other titles, too, but since I have not seen most of them, I shall not take the risk of mentioning the books.

Why have these stories stayed buried in the files of *The Listener* for half a century, and how were they dusted off and brought into the light? *Behind the Screen* was broadcast first in six installments, with each contributor reading his own piece. The competition included was set after the fifth installment, and it was followed by a debate between Dorothy L. Sayers and Anthony Berkeley on "Plotting a Detective Story." Sayers had been responsible for organizing this serial. She was then asked to arrange another, and the more ambitious *The Scoop* was the result.

Their reappearance now is owed to the zest and pertinacity of a publisher's traveller, who

uses his spare time to search out relics of the
criminal past in secondhand bookshops. His re-
searches involved old magazines as well as
books. He discovered the existence of these
broadcasts, and told Livia Gollancz of the Victor
Gollancz publishing firm about them. Livia
approached the very active Dorothy L. Sayers
Historical and Literary Society—and lo, they
were able to provide the full texts.

The club's activities have varied over the
years. Before World War II it had rooms in central
London, where members could meet. During the
war years, no new members were elected, although there may have been informal dinners.
After the war it again had for a few years a room
where occasional meetings were held. For several years it was in the doldrums, with meetings
attended by very few members. More recently is
has flourished again, with the decision to confine
activities to three dinners a year. Two of these
are held at the famous Garrick Club, and the
third, at which new members are initiated, at the
Café Royal. The Garrick dinners are always fully
booked, and the initiation dinner, which has been
held at the Café Royal for more than thirty years,
includes the ceremony for which the club is famous.

The ceremony is said to have been devised by
G. K. Chesterton and Dorothy L. Sayers. It consists of a ritual spoken mostly by the president,
with responses made by the initiate, who has to
name something that he or she holds sacred in
relation to crime fiction. The ritual has been
changed over the years as the club's membership
altered: it was, for example, absurd to ask of Dick

Francis or Geoffrey Household, whose works contain little or no detection: "Do you promise that
your detectives shall well and truly detect?"

The procedure, however, remains very much
as it was. After dinner the lights are turned out.
The president enters, followed by the other members, who light his progress by candles. The secretary bears Eric the Skull on a bed of black velvet. The president recites the ritual, in which
nowadays two or three members take part; an en-
comium is pronounced on the candidate's works
by the proposer. The candidate places a hand
upon Eric the Skull, whose eyes light up, swears
allegiance to the club's unwritten laws, and is
elected by acclamation. The president then pro-
nounces a blessing (although a qualified one),
which did not exist in the original version of the
ritual:

> You are duly elected a member of the
>   Detection Club,
> and if you fail to remember your promises
>   and break even
> one of our unwritten rules,
> may other writers anticipate your plots
> may total strangers sue you for libel
> may your pages swarm with misprints
> and your sales continually diminish.
> But should you, as no doubt you will,
>   recall these promises
> and observe the rules,
> may reviewers rave over you
> and literary editors lunch you
> may book clubs bargain for you
> and women's magazines carve you up

> may films be made from you (and keep
>   your plots)
> and American universities embalm you.

The position of president, or as it was origi-
nally called, Ruler, is held until the president
dies or resigns. No president has resigned. The
club has had only a few presidents in its rather
more than half century of life and, remarkably,
the black scarlet-lined cloak worn for the initiation ceremony has fitted them all. They have
been G. K. Chesterton, from the year of the first
dinner to 1936; E. C. Bentley from 1936 to 1949;
Dorothy L. Sayers from 1949 to 1958; Agatha
Christie from 1958 to 1976 (with the assistance
from 1958 to 1963 of Lord Gorell, who because
of Mrs. Christie's extreme shyness, undertook to
propose toasts and make introductory speeches),
and since 1976—

Julian Symons

THE SCOOP

dorothy l. sayers, agatha christie, e. c. bentley, anthony berkeley, freeman wills crofts, and clemence dane

I

OVER THE WIRE

by dorothy l. sayers

The offices of that irrepressible daily, the *Morning Star*, were humming with the usual hub-bub incidental to six o'clock in the evening of November 9. Hemingway, the news-editor, the final court of appeal in the hurly-burly, sat under the shaded lights in the news-room, making up the final news-pages. The Lord Mayor's Show would take the banner headline and leading column on the first page, with a photograph, of course. The Newcastle exhumation case had proved disappointing—the analyst had failed to find any poison in the body. Impossible to get more than a brief par out of that. Well then, No. 5 column had better take the story about Archbishop Denounces Companionate Marriage—unless, of course, something turned up at the last minute in connection with the Lone Bungalow Mystery.

In the managerial departments the pressure was not quite so great. Miss Beryl Blackwood, the manager's secretary, had found time to dart away to the cloakroom to powder a very pugnacious, tip-tilted, but thoroughly attractive nose. Meeting

9

Miss Irene Timmins, her fellow-secretary, similarly engaged, she relaxed her usual business-like attitude so far as to indulge in a little gossip.

"I see they've put your Mr. Johnson on to this Lone Bungalow story," said Miss Timmins. "Have you got any vanishing-cream, dear?"

"In my locker," said Miss Blackwood, "but please do not call him *my* Mr. Johnson. He's not my property."

"Isn't he?" said Miss Timmins, "I should have said he was — but no doubt, dear, you know best. But I must say I was a bit surprised at Mr. Hemingway putting Mr. Johnson on to that story. I mean, he's a bit young isn't he? I mean, he hasn't had the same experience as Mr. Oliver has. If you ask me, I'd say Mr. Oliver had ought to have gone down to the Jumbles, not Mr. Johnson."

"Mr. Oliver was on the Newcastle exhumation," said Miss Blackwood, quietly, though perhaps with a slight quickening of interest in her voice.

"Yes, but that's a wash-out. Anyway, what was it? Only a dull old man of eighty-four. Stands to reason it was time he popped off, any old how. But this Lonely Bungalow at the Jumbles — that's the kind of crime that interests me, if you understand what I mean. That poor girl found there all alone, stabbed through the heart — I mean, it sort of brings it home to one. Why, it might have been you or me."

"The moral is," said Miss Blackwood, lightly, "if you can't be good, be careful."

"That's just what I say," agreed Miss Timmins. "Even if this fellow Tracey *was* her husband — and if he was, he was a funny sort of husband by all accounts, only coming down weekends and never turning up or writing or anything when he knew she'd been killed – still, give him the benefit of the doubt. But if he *was* her husband, what was she doing with this other fellow, what's his name, Fisher? He was down there on Saturday night when she was killed, wasn't he? And what business had he got to be about the place at all, I should like to know, and her alone in the bungalow without so much as a charwoman?"

"Fisher must know more than he says," said Miss Blackwood.

"'Course he knows something!" retorted Miss Timmins. "Shouldn't wonder if he knows all about it. Daresay he did it, if the truth was known. The nasty beast! You can tell by his photograph. He's one of that fat, smooth kind. I shouldn't wonder if he'd done Tracey in as well. That would account for Tracey not turning up, wouldn't it? You mark my words. One of these days we'll be hearing of Tracey's body being found somewhere with a knife in its back or something, same as the girl."

"There was no knife in the girl's back," corrected Miss Blackwood.

"Well, I mean a knife-wound, or a dagger-wound, or whatever it was. You needn't take me up so quick – you know what I mean. Well, what I say is, it isn't worth it. Once a girl goes off the rails it's sure to lead to trouble. And my word! If I was going to do it, I'd do it properly and see I got a flat in Park Lane or a villa on the Riviera or something. It gives me the shudders to think of that horrid little bungalow, miles away from anywhere, as lonely as sin, and damp, too, I shouldn't wonder. Me for the bright lights. Well, I hope your Mr. Johnson – sorry, *our* Mr. Johnson – makes something of it. But I still think they ought to have sent Mr. Oliver. Well, I must fly, dear. Ta so much for the vanishing cream."

Miss Blackwood went upstairs again and sat down to file some correspondence. She worked away in comparative quiet till 6:45, when the manager departed to get his evening meal. She was preparing to follow his example when the phone rang, and she stopped to answer it.

"Hullo! Yes – this is Extension 148 – Manager's office – Yes, Miss Blackwood speaking – Who? – Mr. Johnson – where are you speaking from? – What – the Jumbles? – oh, are you? Have you got a – You have? – a real scoop? – Oh, well done! – I can't hear you – Yes, isn't this line awful? – You found *what*? pepper? – Oh! the *weapon*? – Oh good! – I didn't get that – you think you can identify it? – Oh! how – Yes – where? – Yes, I heard that – you think you saw it in a shop-window but where? – Broad Street? – What? – Look here, hold on a minute and I'll get them to change the line – I say, Exchange! can you do anything about this line? it sounds like a machine-gun barrage – Ah! Yes, thank you, *much* better – now Mr. Johnson, say it again – Yes, I've got it now – Yes – Yes – What does Mr. Hemingway say about it? – *What*? Not been through to Mr. Hemingway? But my good lad, you musn't waste your time talking to me – No – no – certainly not – the idea – of course you must go straight through to Mr. Hemingway – what? – no – no, I can't – no. Mr. Johnson, please don't talk nonsense – I am not your darling – Don't be so ridiculous – I am putting you through – I say, Switchboard! Switchboard! – Please put this Brighton call through to Mr. Hemingway's office – Yes – I'm hanging up now – Right-oh!"

Miss Blackwood slammed the receiver down. Young Johnson was getting a bit of a nuisance. But fancy his picking up a scoop like that. Actually finding the missing weapon! And such a piece of luck his being able to identify it, too. All the same, it was rather unfair that Mr. Oliver shouldn't have been given the chance. She sighed a little as she put on her hat and coat.

In the meantime the call had been switched through to the news-editor's office. Hemingway, alert and abrupt as ever, his eternal cigarette clamped into the corner of his mouth, barked briefly into the receiver.

"Yes? – who's that – Johnson? – Yes – Oh, you have? that's good – what is it? – Have you got the man? – Oh! – You've got the weapon? – Where? – What's it like? – You think *what*? – Identify it? How? Don't waste time – Yes? – Oh! here, hold on a moment."

He drew a pad towards him and again turned to the telephone.

"Johnson! – just give me that story briefly – Yes – Yes – Yes – Yes – Can you remember the name of the shop? – Oh – well, perhaps it will come to you presently – Now, look here, of course you haven't told anybody about this? -- Right – Watkins, get me a time-table. Thanks. Hullo. Johnson! Where are you speaking from? The pub? How long will it take you to get back to Brighton? – Oh, I see – Well, I think you'd better come straight on up to town. Bring the weapon

with you and write your story up on the way. Can
you catch the 7:35? – H'm – well, if you miss that,
there's the 8:35 – gets in 9:48 – that'd do. I'll see
that everything's waiting for you this end – Right
– I'm going off, but Mr. Redman will have it all
in hand – Right – Right – Right you are. Goodbye."

He scribbled furiously on a sheet of paper and
rang violently for the foreman-printer, who presently came galloping in, festooned with trailing
galley-sheets.

"Oh, here, Bill, Mr. Johnson will be coming in
later with a story about the Jumbles Bungalow
Murder. I shall want two columns on the front
page for a big scoop. Cut the Lord Mayor out of
the banner-line and push all that stuff over to columns 5, 6 and 7 and the photograph on to page
2. Perks, I shall want a photographer and the
block-makers to stand by for an urgent rush job.
Is Simmonds in the office? Fetch him, somebody.
Now, you've got all that clear? Right. Mr. Redman
will see to anything else that turns up. Oh, Simmonds – here's a story Johnson has 'phoned up
. . . Jumbles murder – he's found the weapon –
here are the details – Get out a banner-head and
a bunch of two-column captions and let Bill have
them, will you? Johnson will be up here with the
weapon and the rest of the dope in an hour or
two, I hope – before ten at latest."

The subordinate trotted dutifully away. Hemingway glanced at the clock.

"Five past seven. Let's hope he catches the
7:35. Well, that's that. Where's that story about
the Railway Crash?"

At 7:25 a slight calm supervened and Hemingway rose to go home. The night news-editor had not yet made his appearance; in his absence Hemingway turned to the chief sub and handed over to him the notes which he had scribbled down at the telephone.

"Give Mr. Redman this when he comes in," he said. "You see, Johnson says he thinks he can identify the weapon from having seen it in a shop. Unfortunately, he can't recollect the name of the firm or we might have tried to get an inquiry through tonight, but it may be possible to do something about it when he comes in. I'll have to be off now. Carry on."

Mr. Redman, the night news-editor, came briskly into the office a little after ten. He had looked in at 7:30 to find out how matters stood for the evening, and, learning that Johnson was not expected to arrive with his story for some little time, had gone out again, leaving a message that he was to be found at the Chesire Cheese. He now ran through the reports submitted to him, and then said, sharply:

"How about this Jumbles story? Where is it?"

"Not in yet," said the chief sub.

"Why not?" said Redman.

"Johnson didn't come by the early train. He'll be on the 9:48 – it starts from Brighton 8:35."

"The 9:48? He should be here by now. Go and find out what has happened to him. He ought to have rung through from the station. See if he's in the reporters' room."

Johnson was not in the reporters' room, nor had he come into the building. The hands of the clock pointed to 10:15. Bill, the foreman-printer, presented himself lugubriously in the news-editor's room.

"What are we to do about this here front page, Mr. Redman? Will it be down soon? We ought to have it on the machines in 'alf an hour."

"Shall I ring through to Victoria?" suggested the chief sub. "Perhaps the train's late. They may be able to tell us when it's expected in."

"Yes, do," said Redman. "If Johnson isn't here in time, we must do what we can with Hemingway's notes." He buzzed, irritably. "Have we got anyone here who can write up the story from what we've got?"

"Mr. Oliver has come in from Newcastle, sir."

"Send him up."

The chief sub succeeded in getting through to Victoria just as Oliver presented himself, a tall red-haired man, untidily dressed – the leading crime-reporter on the *Morning Star*.

"They say," announced the sub, "that the 9:48 was held up and didn't get in till ten, sir."

"Hell!" said Redman. "Well, can't be helped – if he isn't here within the next ten minutes, Oliver, you'll have to do your best with it. Here you are – dagger found in a hollow tree; Johnson thinks it came from a shop in Bond Street. Spin it out as well as you can. We must do without the photograph, and — Hullo! perhaps that's Johnson."

The telephone was ringing again, violently. He caught it up, and listened, then turned cheerfully to Oliver. "That was Victoria Station. They've found a corpse in a telephone-booth. There may be a story in it. Better go down and see, Oliver. Get down to it quickly and 'phone through at once."

Oliver hastened away.

Twenty minutes past ten; five and twenty past; half past.

Then the telephone began again in the news-room – loudly, insistently.

"Yes — *Morning Star* — news-editor here — who's that?"

"Oliver speaking from Victoria. The dead man in the telephone booth is Johnson. Stabbed in the back. Just over the heart. Same sort of wound as in the Jumbles murder. His notes have been sto-len and so has the weapon he was bringing with him. There was no weapon on the body, either. The murderer must have followed him and killed him to suppress his evidence. I am carrying on."

"Good God!" said Redman. "Johnson's killed. The Jumbles murderer has got him."

He paused for a moment in a sort of conster-nation. Then the journalist's ruling instinct took the upper hand. His fingers flew to the buzzers.

"Well, that's our story. Send Simmonds up at once. Tell the comps to stand by. Peters, take this down."

He dictated the story, urgently, eagerly, trium-phantly. The caption-writer's pencil flew over the paper, roughing out the headlines:

"Morning Star" Reporter Stabbed

Jumbles Murderer Loose in London

Slays Journalist to Suppress Damning Clue

Porter Finds Body in Telephone Box

Redman nodded. "Get this down – push it along

– send Bill up here – see if there's a photograph of Johnson in the place. Here, Matthews – go round and get a story from his mother if he's got one. See if he's got a girl. Get her story. Hurry up, there – don't stand about."

Bill, the foreman-printer, stood up in the high gallery, looking down upon the machines that were the pride of his life. The outer sheets, still hot from the foundry, had been trundled through on a truck, lifted upon the cylinders, clamped into place, made ready. It was eleven o'clock. He raised his hand to the switch.

"Ready, down there?"

"Ready."

"Let her go."

The switch clicked down. With a steady and increasing roar the machines sprang to life. The paper reeled out under the rollers. The tall building shivered, throbbed, shuddered into one long thunder of reverberation.

Rumbling and clanking in the pride of their fantastic circulation, two million *Morning Stars* sang together; they shouted for joy. They had got their scoop, after all.

II

AT THE INQUEST

by agatha christie

The inquest on Geraldine Tracey was held on the morning of Wednesday, November 11. Oliver, untidy as ever, his aged hat jammed down over his eyes, chose his position with care. Near at hand was a stout, middle-aged woman and a thin, acidulated friend. Before now Oliver had found the comments of interested outsiders helpful. The stout woman was of the kind that by doubting everything, and discounting every remark firmly, inflamed the second type to frenzied volubility.

"That's the witnesses over there," said the stout lady. "That's Fisher, that is. The one that used to take her out in his car. Looks bloated, doesn't he?"

"That's not Fisher," said the friend. "I saw Fisher's photograph in the paper this morning. That's not him."

"Don't you think you know everything, Maria. You'd doubt an angel, you would. That's him.

Look – he's biting his nails. Always shows a nasty temper in a man, so they say."

"He looks pasty," said the friend.

"And well he may do. He knows what folk are saying about him. Looks a little like a slug, doesn't he? The kind you find in your salad that gives you quite a turn. My niece by marriage married a man looking rather like that – and now I come to think of it, she died sudden – bad pork pie they said it was. I wonder now –"

Maria shook her head, decidedly.

"He's no murderer."

"Now – how do you know?"

However, at this point the proceedings opened, and the two ladies were silent, leaning their necks forward and breathing hard in the ecstasy of suspense.

After the necessary preliminaries, the first witness was called, a figure of almost impossible elegance in black, wearing a small round of black velvet apparently attached to the back of her head by suction.

"You are Mary Evans?"

In answer to the Coroner, she said her name was Mary Evans and she carried on a millinery business under the name of Madame Evanalda. She had identified the deceased, whom she had employed as Geraldine Potts and who had left her three months previously. As far as she knew the deceased was not married, and she never heard her mention any relations except a brother.

The foreman of the jury intimated that he would like to ask a question.

"Did you consider her to be a virtuous girl?"

"Really!" Madame Evanalda seemed at a loss to deal with a question put in such Victorian language. "Really, I do not know what you mean. Miss Potts behaved with perfect propriety during business hours. I should not dream of countenancing anything else."

"And out of business hours?"

"That is hardly my province. I know nothing – nothing whatever."

Madame Evanalda was dismissed – an elegant withdrawal. Henry Vaughan Fisher was called. There was no doubt about it – Fisher was not showing to advantage.

"These smug fellows get rattled easily," thought Oliver.

He could visualise Fisher a shrewd and prosperous figure in his business, respected for his foresight and acumen. Cheap jewellery in Birmingham had laid the foundations of his fortune. Again he could see Mr. Fisher a genial host at supper at the Savoy, flushed and amiable, very conscious of who was paying for the champagne. A generous, sporty "good fellow," who nevertheless usually got value for his money. Was there a third Fisher? A jealous lover who stabbed to kill? In this world, thought Oliver, nothing is impossible. . . .

The Coroner was helping Mr. Fisher very kindly through his evidence. Oliver, with his experience, knew well enough what that meant. The police did not want Mr. Fisher upset. On the surface his story was to be accepted absolutely.

Yes, Mr. Fisher had gone over on Saturday to see Mrs. Tracey. Her husband, he understood,

was to be away. He looked apprehensive, but
there was nothing to fear. No awkward questions
were asked.

No, he had never met Mr. Tracey. Mr. Tracey
was, he believed, a commercial traveller.

Led by the Coroner, he went on to narrate the
events of Saturday evening. He had come by car,
arriving at the Bungalow about nine o'clock. He
had knocked and rung, but without eliciting any
response. Finally, growing annoyed, he had
thought of trying the door. To his great surprise
it was open. He had entered and switched on the
lights. He passed straight from the little lobby
into the sitting-room. Here, to his horror, he almost stumbled over the body of Mrs. Tracey. She
had, he was convinced, been dead some time.

"And then, Mr. Fisher?" said the Coroner
suavely.

"Well – after a bit, I – I drove back to Brighton."

Fisher mopped his forehead.

"Shame!" said the stout lady. Others agreed
with her.

"Silence, if you please," said the Coroner
sternly.

"You did not communicate with the police
until later?" he went on.

"No."

"Quite so."

Fisher stumbled into speech. "It has been a
great shock to me – a great shock. I've got a weak
heart –" ("Drink," murmured the stout lady.) "A
very weak heart. I – I drove about a long time
and thought over what was best to be done."

"Quite so," said the Coroner again. Into those two words he put all the censure he was able to put. He bitterly regretted the limitations imposed by the police.

"You did eventually communicate with the police, Mr. Fisher?"

"Yes, I – I – in the end – about midnight – I rang them up."

"Quite so," said the Coroner for the third time and with an expressiveness improved by practice. He sighed. "That will be all, Mr. Fisher."

Police evidence followed. As the result of a telephone call, the local police had arrived at the bungalow some time after one o'clock.

Gladys Sharp then gave evidence.

"You were maidservant to the deceased?"

"No, I was a daily help," said Miss Sharp coldly.

"You had been employed at the bungalow – how long?"

"Couple of months."

"And you were the last person to see Mrs. Tracey alive?"

"Well, what if I was?"

"Kindly answer the questions put to you. When did you last see the deceased?"

"Three o'clock. I was going off as usual."

"That was the time you usually left?"

"No – earlier as a rule, but she wanted a bit of extra cooking done for the weekend and I had to get it all ready before I left."

"You were not to come again till the Monday morning, was that it?"

Miss Sharp winked in a vulgar manner.

"What do *you* think? I should have been *dee trow*, as they say."

"Kindly answer the questions put to you in a proper manner."

"Oh! very well."

"Was that the usual arrangement?"

"Whenever she had a little game on, yes."

The Coroner seemed minded to protest once more, then evidently considered it better to let Miss Sharp give evidence in her own way.

"A guest was expected for the weekend?"

"Yes."

"Did Mrs. Tracey mention who it was?"

"She said it was her husband – but that was all my eye."

"What exactly do you mean?"

"Well, either way it was all my eye. I knew it was Mr. Fisher coming: she would not have taken the pains she did for Tracey. And if it were Tracey coming, that would not have made him her husband. I could tell you –"

"Please confine yourself to answering my questions. Now have you any definite knowledge that Mr. and Mrs. Tracey were not married?"

"I don't suppose I have got any what you call definite knowledge. But I know what is what, don't I? Gentlemen who only come down for weekends and call themselves commercial travellers. Funny kind of husband – I –"

"That will do, please. Now you last saw Mrs. Tracey at three o'clock you say. Was her manner much as usual?"

"Pretty near."

"She was not worried or upset in any way?"

"No – the opposite. Manicuring her nails she was when I left and going to get all togged up. Oh! I knew Mr. Fisher was coming all right."

"When did you first hear of what had occurred?"

"Next day. My Auntie told me. Her husband brought the news home from the Cat and Fence. You could have knocked me down with a feather. 'What,' I said – 'murdered?' –"

"Thank you, Miss Sharp, that will do."

None too pleased at being cut short just when she was getting under way, Miss Sharp stood down.

The medical evidence closed the proceedings. It was brief and technical. As understood by the lay mind, the deceased had been stabbed by a sharp instrument with a triangular blade and the heart had been penetrated. The wound could not have been self-inflicted. The doctor could express no opinion as to the weapon. Nothing of the kind had been found. He had examined the body about 1:30 a.m. Death had occurred four to six hours previously. It was impossible to say exactly.

The inquest was thereupon adjourned for a week.

Many people besides Beryl Blackwood had recognised the fact that Oliver had "a way with him." In this case, the lady to fall under the spell was Miss Gladys Sharp.

She herself could never quite remember how it came about that, anxious as she was to talk to anyone who would listen, she had nevertheless permitted herself to be isolated from many would-be listeners, and shortly afterwards found herself accepting hospitality in the Lido Café seated at a small table opposite this friendly red-haired young man.

Oliver sized up Miss Sharp and ordered tea, crumpets, muffins, French pastries, and, after consultation, two mysterious confections called Morning Glory and Chocolate Fudge Delight.

As Miss Sharp fixed her teeth in a virulent-looking green iced cake, Oliver opened the conversation.

"Extraordinary show today," said Oliver. "I thought that Coroner didn't know his business. You might have given very valuable evidence which he suppressed – deliberately suppressed."

"That's what I thought myself," said Miss Sharp. "Shutting me up like that! If I'd told all *I* knew –" She nodded her head several times.

"Ah!" said Oliver. "Your kind doesn't. You're reticent by nature, I could see that at once."

"I don't know how you know – but that's quite true. All along, you know, I've had my doubts about those two. Always sent away for the week-end – and Oh! the state of the place on Monday morning! Not so much as a teaspoon washed up. Everything piled in the kitchen sink. The airs she gave herself!"

"Very trying," said Oliver. "What was Tracey like to look at?"

"I only saw him once. Just an ordinary looking fellow."

"Like me?"

"You're one for a joke. Like you, indeed! I'd know you anywhere by the carrots! Ginger for pluck, they say. But him – Tracey, I mean – well, he looked just like anyone else."

"Dark or fair?"

"Oh, sort of darkish."

"Tall or short?"

"Kind of middling."

"What colour were his eyes?"

"Blue, I think – no, I believe they were brown. Really, I can't remember. I never got close enough," she giggled.

"Have another of these things," said Oliver, handing the plate.

Well, really, I don't mind if I do." She accepted an éclair.

"I suppose," said Oliver, "his ears didn't stick out, or he didn't walk with a limp, or anything like that?"

"No," said Gladys. "But he had a moustache," she added helpfully.

"Ye-es," said Oliver. "But then shaving is so cheap, isn't it? Seems rather odd he hasn't come forward, don't you think?"

"Not he!"

"You mean –?"

"I mean – he did it, of course. Who else could have done it?"

"Well – what about our friend Fisher? The Man on the Spot."

"Mr. Fisher's a nice gentleman."

"Ah!" said Oliver, mentally visualising a pound note passing from palm to palm. "Yes, of course."

"Tracey murdered her all right. They were having rows, you know. At it hammer and tongs, I should say. Not that I actually heard anything, but she'd let on a thing or two on Monday morn-

ings. Men expected to have it all their own way
– shut a girl up in a lonely hole far from anywhere
– that sort of thing. No, he came down that day
and they had a row and he did her in. From what
she said, he was a jealous sort of fellow."

"Well," said Oliver. "Perhaps you're right.
Woman's intuition and all that. And yet I've
got a fancy myself for Tracey as a corpse. Turning up in a lonely spot on the downs. The third
murder —"

"Morning Glory," said the waitress, putting a
U in the word "Morning" by implication.

Oliver gazed with fascinated horror at a con-
coction of pink and white ice cream, a chunk of
pineapple, two or three raspberries, some chocolate syrup, some nuts, a coy bit of banana and
the remnants of yesterday's plates of stewed
prunes.

"No wonder," he murmured, "that women
have intuition. They need it."

"Mr. Oliver, you're not eating anything."

"I'm on a diet," said Oliver hastily. "I suppose," he went on thoughtfully, "that living at the
bungalow must have been very lonely."

"It would have given *me* the creeps all right,"
said Miss Sharp. "You've got to walk to the 'bus
– and the 'bus only goes every hour. All told, it
takes you three-quarters of an hour to get to Brighton. I ask you! No wonder she got the pip. Men
are selfish, you can't get away from it. Taking a
girl far away from her friends and expecting her
to be grateful stuck down with nothing to do all
day. Naturally, she took up with Mr. Fisher. Ah!
well," sighed Miss Sharp, "I don't blame her."

"That's very nice of you."

"Of course the place not being respectable, I oughtn't to have stayed. But I've always been one for good nature. I put up with a lot though. Why this very last Friday afternoon she went on at me like a fishwife just because I was trying an ornamental jade-headed pin that she'd got in my hair. What was the harm in that, I'd like to know? Anyway, I thought she'd gone out."

"Too bad," said Oliver. "You must know a lot about human nature. What was your last mistress like?"

"Catsby, her name was. Cat by name and cat by nature. I —"

"Chocolate Delight," said the waitress menacingly.

"Looks good, doesn't it?" said Gladys.

Oliver shuddered. Never, he thought, had he seen anything so revolting.

"Catsby," said Oliver, averting his eyes. "Let me see, are those the Catsbys in Monmouth Drive?"

"No, Mrs. Walter C., 18 Maidstone Avenue. As I was saying — what was I saying?"

At this moment Oliver decided to spring from his chair with a sharp exclamation.

"Good gracious," he exclaimed, examining his wrist. "I've entirely forgotten a most important appointment, Miss Sharp. Will you forgive me if I rush away? It's been such a delightful time."

"That's all right," said Gladys, still further benign under the influence of the Chocolate Delight.

Oliver pressed money upon the mournful waitress and left the Lido Café hastily. There were several things he wanted to do before returning to London.

He started by making a call at Maidstone Avenue and was fortunate enough to obtain an interview with Mrs. Catsby. Hastily inventing an invalid sister, Oliver pressed for details of Gladys Sharp.

Mrs. Catsby, a monumental lady, was impressive.

"Dangerous — most dangerous. I don't mind saying so to *you*, Mr. Oliver. The girl talks, you know. *Talks*."

Oliver said he had guessed as much.

"And if you check her, she turns nasty. Vindictive. Several most curious occurrences. Petty spite. A gas fire left on all night — mere wicked spite to increase our gas bill. And she broke several of my favourite ornaments on purpose. One can prove nothing, of course. Also, I myself have very grave doubts whether the girl is really respectable. I have seen her myself walking with very strange looking men. And look where she has been last! Perhaps she concealed the fact from your sister. *At the Lonely Bungalow*, Mr. Oliver. I ask you, would a nice girl get herself mixed up with a murder case? As to honesty," went on Mrs. Catsby rapidly without giving Oliver time to answer her last query, "I must confess that I never actually missed anything. But nothing would surprise me! Nothing! She said the most impertinent things to me."

"In fact," said Oliver, "she is not to be relied upon?"

"I made it my practice," said Mrs. Catsby, "never to believe a word she said. That is my invariable custom with servants — and I have a wide experience. I am continually changing."

"Quite so," said Oliver. "Very natural."

"Goodbye," said Mrs. Catsby, shaking hands. "I'm so glad you called personally. With a written character I should, of course, have had to say she was honest, trustworthy and reliable. The tongue is mightier than the pen, Mr. Oliver."

"I'm beginning to believe it is," said Oliver and made his escape.

Before returning to London he paid a visit to the scene of the crime – deserted at this late hour of the evening. As Gladys had said, it was a lonely spot.

He identified without difficulty the hollow tree in which Johnson had made his sensational discovery. A thousand pities that he had not described it in detail over the telephone! But it seemed he had rung up from the nearest pub and had naturally said as little as possible in case of being overheard.

Had he been overheard? Or had somebody seen him actually find the thing?

Oliver looked round with a slight shiver. The Bungalow itself was only a few hundred yards distant. He walked towards it. Suddenly he caught his breath. Dimly outlined, he saw the figure of a man trying to force the catch of one of the windows. Noiselessly the reporter sprinted across the grass. The man started and wheeled round. Oliver flashed his torch full in the other's face. He saw a man of middle-age, clean-shaven, with an ugly scar running down one cheek.

"Who the Hell are you?" the man snarled.

"What the Hell are you doing trying to break in at that window?" returned Oliver.

The man started – then laughed unpleasantly. "And why not, I should like to know? I've more right here than you have, I bet. This bungalow was Geraldine Tracey's. And I'm her brother – Arthur Potts. What the Hell have you got to say to that?"

III

FISHER'S ALIBI

by e. c. bentley

On the morning following the inquest at Brighton, Oliver, the leading crime reporter, was again in the office of the *Morning Star*, deep in discussion of the crime with Hemingway, the newseditor. At this time of day, a little before noon, the office was comparatively peaceful. Hemingway had already dispatched a score of reporters on various missions; quarrelled bitterly over the telephone with a news agency and a firm of photographers whose work had (so he said) let the paper down disastrously; listened grimly to some acid remarks, also over the telephone, from the principal proprietor; and interviewed several persons offering to place at his disposal information that was almost, but not quite, priceless. He was now pacing the room in his usual restless way, and in the big ashtray on his table the foundations of the daily pile of cigarette-ends were already well and truly laid.

"Well, what about this Potts?" he snapped; for
Oliver had now come to this point in his narrative
of the doings of the day before. "Said he was her
brother, huh! It sounds to me!" For Hemingway
had worked on newspapers in the Western States,
and his speech still bore traces of that experience.

"I thought so, too," Oliver said, "but what he
told me sounded reasonable enough. He said he
was a steward on the boat-service that runs every
night from Southampton to le Havre, and he gave
me his address in Southampton – of course, he
saw the way I'd caught him needed a bit of explaining. He hadn't heard of his sister for some
years, he said, until that same afternoon, when
he was in Brighton on business. He had read a
report of the inquest in the afternoon paper, and
seen there that the murdered Mrs. Tracey's
maiden name was Geraldine Potts: and he knew
his sister had been working at the Evanalda shop.
So he had walked out to the bungalow, he said,
to see if there was anyone there who could tell
him anything; and he didn't deny that he had
been trying to get in to have a look round the
place. Then he said he would have to be getting
back to Brighton at once to catch the 7:15 for
Southampton, as his boat was leaving at eleven
o'clock, and he didn't make any objection when
I said I would walk back with him. We talked on
the way, and I made certain he knew all about
the stewarding job and the run to le Havre, which
I know very well myself."

"Yes," Hemingway grunted, "and you could
have pitched just the same tale as he did, if you'd
been in his shoes. How did you verify it?"

"Well, I saw him go off in the train he had mentioned," Oliver said. "Then I got the railway company's office at Southampton harbour on the 'phone and said I was trying to get in touch with a steward on one of the boats called Potts, and should be much obliged if they could help me. So they told me his name – Arthur – and his address, which was what he'd told me, and they said he was working on the boat leaving at eleven that night. And so I didn't worry any further about friend Potts. He was rather a slimy sort of devil, I thought, but his story was absolutely right, and he was the steward all over."

Hemingway frowned considerably. "I expect you're right," he said. "Anyway, we don't want Potts in this case. It's a perfectly plain one, and we mustn't get it all balled up with mysterious brothers unless we've got to. Of course, Fisher is the man – you can see it sticking out about nine years, and then some. The tale he told – did you ever hear anything so raw? Didn't report to the police at once on finding the body – oh, no! Mr. Fishy Fisher had a little thinking to do first. He had to get the dope he was going to hand out into decent shape."

"I know," Oliver said. "I know that is how it looks. But one has to be guided by the impression people make, to some extent, and I don't believe that Fisher had it in him. You know, Hemingway, when you were a sleuth-hound yourself, and beating everybody else at the game, you always used to say that you didn't give a damn what the evidence against a man was if you just knew he wasn't guilty."

Hemingway smiled a rather sour smile. "True enough," he said, "I always used to play my hunches, and generally they used to win out. But for one thing, I don't believe I ever banked against a case so strong as the case against Fisher is, with really nobody else under suspicion; and for another thing – well, my boy, you won't mind my saying that I'm not quite so confident about your hunches as I used to be about my own."

"But why nobody else under suspicion?" Oliver exclaimed. "I should say that poisonous Gladys Sharp, the maidservant, was a little under suspicion – I was telling you so just now – and she wouldn't be the first domestic to make away with a mistress with whom she lived alone in the house, as we both know. And she was, I told you, so very anxious to insist on it that the dead woman's husband, Tracey, must be the murderer. And of course, apart from her rubbing it in so, there's a lot to be said for him as the criminal; he's much more under suspicion than anyone, to my mind."

Hemingway laughed shortly. "How do you make that out?" he said. "Tracey, or anyone who might have been Tracey, wasn't seen at the place before or after the crime; he was away most of the time, so the girl told you; as a travelling man he might have been a hundred miles away; and the mere fact that Fisher was to be there that weekend shows that Tracey wasn't going to be. What's the answer to all that?"

"I don't know," Oliver said. "We generally start by not knowing things in a crime mystery, don't we? But now tell me what is the answer to this. It's now four clear days after the murder, and all the papers have been full of it, yet the victim's husband hasn't come forward."

"That's not very surprising," Hemingway snapped. "If he was really the husband of somebody else, which is what it looks like, he wouldn't be anxious to be mixed up in the affair, I should say."

At this point the desk-telephone shrilled. Hemingway turned to attend to it, and within fifteen seconds had terminated his conversation with an unknown someone by telling him he could take five guineas or go to the devil, whichever he pleased.

Oliver resumed the discussion. "I can't see why we are to suppose that Tracey wasn't her husband. Nobody has ever suggested he wasn't except the spiteful, nasty-minded little Sharp rat I was stuffing with cakes yesterday. And whether they were married or not, look at the motive Tracey had if he had got to know about Fisher! Murdering a wife or mistress by reason of jealousy is no rare thing nowadays; and besides, it's the only smell of a motive for the crime that suggests itself, as far as we've got."

Hemingway shrugged impatiently. "You're putting talk against facts," he said. "What we do know is that Fisher's conduct after his alleged finding of the body at the bungalow was thoroughly suspicious. We know he lives in Brighton. We know that poor Johnson made his discovery of the weapon and perhaps got hold of other evidence. We know that nothing would have been easier than for the murderer to wait at the station in Brighton for Johnson, travel by the same train, and arrive with him in London at the terminus where Johnson was killed. We know that much, and it looks a lot to me. What I want you to do is to get after Fisher right away, and find out about his movements on the night when Johnson was done in. He must have a story, of course; and the police must have got his story, since anyone connected with the first crime is suspected of both. And it must be a story that holds together, or Fisher would hardly be at liberty now. Find out what that story is, Oliver – and bust it!"

At four o'clock that afternoon Oliver was seeking for the establishment of Mr. Fisher's firm in North Street, Brighton. It was not hard to find, and if it was not the best jeweller's shop in Brighton it looked, Oliver told himself, as if it thought it was. Its window glass and all external appointments were obviously expensive, and although there was the show of cheap and hideous trinkets to be looked for in a seaside resort, these were cast aside into the shade by the display of more solid and stately wares. The place gave somehow the impression of an old-established and very sound concern, and Oliver reflected that, if Mr. Fisher was the moving spirit in its fortunes, he thoroughly knew his business.

Oliver stopped at a neighbouring newspaper-stand and purchased an unneeded evening paper. Finding an opening for conversation with the vendor presented no difficulty to an expert. Forming at a glance a very definite opinion as to the kind of thing in which the fattish and furtive-looking young man would be intrested, Oliver turned to the stop-press Turf news, and, after a brief glance, swore convincingly. He next studied "Gaffer Grey's" prophecies for the next day's racing and, looking up, caught the vendor's sympathetic eye.

"D'you know anything?" inquired Oliver in a low tone. The flattered youth winked portentously.

"The 2:15 tomorrow," he replied. "It's a cinch for Limpin' Lucifer – it'll come 'ome alone," and at once he and Oliver were deep in the young man's favourite subject. Soon Oliver turned the conversation.

"That jeweller's shop, Fisher and Flensburger," he said. "Is that the Fisher who gave evidence at the inquest?"

The young man was quite ready to talk about Fisher, for whom he betrayed no little admiration. Fisher, it appeared, shared the young man's fondness for what he called sport, and must, it was thought, do very well at it. He had from time to time given the young man a tip that had "clicked." The firm was highly prosperous, and was believed to do a little discreet money-lending as a side-line. Fisher was a popular character with all those who did not mind a chap's being a man of the world – by which, it was evident, the young man meant a loose liver. Nobody had been surprised to hear of Fisher having been friendly with a married woman – she wasn't, said the young man darkly, the first – but for his being under suspicion of the crime, nobody who knew the man could consider that for a moment. Everybody knew Fisher would not hurt a fly; he was kindheartedness itself. Besides, where would be the sense of it? What would Fisher want, going round knifing girls that he happened to be sweet on? It appeared, further, that Fisher was unmarried, and dwelt at Hove in a highly expensive block of flats.

Oliver took a cordial farewell of the communicative young man, and soon afterwards presented his professional card at Fisher and Flensburger's with a request that Mr. Fisher would see him for a few moments.

As Oliver had rather expected, Mr. Fisher was nothing loth. He "saw" Oliver, for more than a few moments.

Fisher was evidently a much-worried man. His rubicund face and slightly waxed moustache would look cheery enough, Oliver thought, at a normal time; but now it was drawn with lines of anxiety, and his eyes told a tale of nervous strain. As he came through the door marked "Private" at the back of the shop, he straightened his rather heavy figure and gave a mechanical touch to his expensive tie-pin. The room into which he led his visitor was of medium size, well kept and smartly furnished, with a gleaming table in the centre and a glass topped knee-hole desk at the window. "My partner uses this room," Fisher explained, "and we see people on private business here. Let's go into my own office behind here, where we can be snug." He opened a door, with upper panels of ground glass, leading to an inner room that was smaller and more homely in appearance; but for the big writing-table it might have been the "den" of a well-to-do citizen not troubled with artistic tastes.

Fisher, after pressing on Oliver an excellent cigar, was quite candid about his motive for welcoming the representative of the *Morning Star*. "I'm under suspicion, I know," he said. "I want the plain truth about my position to be known as widely as possible, and anything your people care to do in making it public I shall be thankful for. Nobody who knows me thinks I had anything to do with these two murders; but there's plenty who don't know me, and I'm being looked at sideways wherever I show my face. It's damn well got on my nerves. Now, as you know, the whole point is what I was doing on the Monday night at the time that poor young chap was followed up to London and murdered – if I didn't do that I didn't do the other."

"Yes," Oliver said. "It's generally agreed that one alibi would do for both crimes."

"All right," Fisher said. "Now the first thing is that Flensburger and I are in negotiation about taking in another partner, and this man wired on Monday, unexpectedly, to say he would be in Brighton on Tuesday morning, and hoped it would be convenient to go into the details of the business then. Well, Flensburger is quicker at figures than I am, but he's abroad on the firm's business, so I had to get out the statement myself – some of our business is too confidential for any but the partners to handle. And by the way," Fisher added, quickly, "that's not for publication."

"Certainly not," agreed Oliver, with a memory of the young man's hint about money-lending.

"I saw I should have to make a night of it here," Fisher went on, "and I rather welcomed the idea, for I thought it would take my mind off that ghastly business of the Saturday night. I got all the books and papers into this room and went to work. When the staff went off at closing time I was alone here, except for the char who comes in to do the cleaning every evening. About seven I phoned to the Royal Cambridge Hotel, just over the way, where I'm very well known, and told the head waiter to send me in a bit of dinner and a half-bottle of Pommery. I ordered a chicken casserole, and a Camembert cheese, to be sent over in an hour's time. When I heard the man come in with the dinner I knocked off work — just at 8:15 that was. I went out and told him to lay the dinner on the big table in the outer office there, and to come and take the things away, but not before nine. We passed a pleasant word or two while he was laying dinner, then he went off, and I sat down to it. When I'd finished I came back into this room again and got on with the job. I heard the chap come in later with the tray and rattle about with the dishes and go off; I didn't notice what time, and I'd told him particularly not to disturb me. But he could see, of course, through the glass of the door that the light was on in here; and my hat and coat were out there lying on the writing-table. Well, that was that. I finished up just about 11:45 and then, feeling I wanted a breath of fresh air, I walked home along the front to my place at Hove. I can't say for certain what time it was when I let myself in, but it would have been round about 12:30, I suppose; and then I had a big drink and went straight to bed, feeling dog-tired. That's the whole story," Fisher concluded, and gazed anxiously at his visitor.

Oliver thought that if Fisher's air of perfect sincerity were not genuine, it was the best imitation he had ever met with. But still —

"It certainly was unfortunate," he said, studying the end of his cigar, "that you told the waiter not to disturb you when he came to take away."

"Don't I know it!" Fisher exclaimed with fervour. "If he'd seen me then nobody would have given a thought to me as the man who travelled on the 8:35 from here to London along with Johnson; and I shouldn't have people looking at me as if I was a leper. But don't you see, Mr. Oliver, what I've told you is good enough to clear me, if you look at it fairly; and that's why I want it to be generally known. This place of mine is a good ten minutes' walk from the station. My car was in the garage, and, of course, if I'd taken a taxi it could have been traced at once. I couldn't possibly have got to the station in time for that train after the waiter had laid my dinner and gone away; it couldn't have been done, unless perhaps I had bolted out the moment he was off the premises, and run all the way – and the days when I could run half a mile uphill are unfortunately over, Mr. Oliver. Besides, there was the char at work in the front entrance at that very time – she must have seen me if I did go. And then there's the dinner. I finished every bit of it, and drank the wine, as the man who took away the things can tell you."

Oliver looked at the anxious face consideringly. He could not think the man was lying. He said briskly, "Well, Mr. Fisher, that is a perfectly straight story. I mustn't take up any more of your time; but I should like to ask one thing. What do the police think of what you've just been telling me?"

"I can only suppose they think it's all right," Fisher replied as both men rose to their feet. "They took our new partner's name and address so that they could check that bit. They cross-examined the charwoman, and as for the waiter, they put him through it for nearly half an hour, he told me afterwards. Tell you what," Fisher added helpfully, "you could talk to him yourself if you like if you look into the Cambridge at dinnertime. He attends to the tables exactly opposite where you go in – a little sharp-faced chap, always on the grin – you can't mistake him. Well, so long, Mr. Oliver. Very glad to have met you. Another cigar? No? Then goodbye, and if there's anything else you think I could tell you come and see me again."

Oliver's fattish friend at the newspaper-stand looked at him with a new respect after witnessing Fisher's effusive handshake at the entrance to the jeweller's shop. "I must say 'e seems fond of yer," observed the young man, dryly, as Oliver paused again by his stand. "You're the police or noospapers, I suppose – must be one or the other."

"I am connected with the Press, like yourself," said Oliver, and the young man's face cleared. "Fisher's all right, as you said," the reporter went on. "We had a long talk. He even told me the firm were taking in another partner."

"So they are," the young man declared. "I know, because the chap was there for over an hour on Toosday morning – come down from London 'e did in a lovely car, wot was parked just round the corner 'ere. The showfer come over to me and 'ad a chat, just like you done – 'e 'ad a fancy for the Manchester – and 'e told me 'is boss was goin' into the business if 'e found it was all right."

Oliver dined an hour later at one of the tables in the Royal Cambridge that Fisher had mentioned. It was early for the meal, and the cheerful little waiter could give him his full attention. There seemed to be no doubt about the time when the tray had been taken over to Fisher's office: and the waiter had returned to take away about a quarter past nine. The light had been on in the inner office; and Fisher's overcoat and hat were lying on the writing table where, as the waiter remarked, you couldn't help seeing them. As for the food and wine, there was nothing left – "All he'd left," said the waiter humorously, "was a half a crown for meself. And you needn't go wondering, sir, like the police did, whether he could have made away with the food somehow in a hurry. All the plates and things had been used regular — a waiter can tell, sir, trust me. Thank you very much, sir. Goodnight sir."

Shut in the hotel telephone-cabinet, Oliver was soon in touch with Redman, the night news-editor, in London. But Redman cut short at once his opening words about the Fisher story. "Get here by the next train and write up the stuff on your way," he said briefly. "You're wanted at this end. The weapon has been found."

IV

THE WEAPON

by agatha christie

"The weapon found?" queried Oliver sharply. "Where?"

"Thrown up on top of the telephone-cabinet at Victoria."

"That's clever," said Oliver appreciatively. "So simple, too. Any fingerprints?"

"The police," said Redman, "aren't exactly taking us into their confidence. They're annoyed about Johnson's keeping that discovery of his to himself. We'll have to use tact. But I rather gather that there are no fingerprints."

"Not likely to be," said Oliver. "The ungloved murderer is becoming extinct as the dodo. Any details as to what the weapon's like?"

"A kind of jade-headed Oriental pin or dagger. Rather unique, I fancy. Come up to town and get busy."

"I will," said Oliver and hung up the receiver.

"An Oriental jade-headed pin" – the words seemed familiar somehow. Seated in the train, he took a shabby notebook from his pocket and on one of the pages wrote: "Oriental" and below it "Bond Street" and below that again: "Try Araby's."

At eleven o'clock the next morning, Miss Beryl Blackwood was rung up. "*Your* Mr. Oliver," murmured Miss Timmins, her fellow-secretary, with a meaning laugh.

"Miss Blackwood speaking," said Beryl.

"Hullo," said Oliver's voice. "This is to report a reverse with heavy loss. The police have rebuffed me. My pleasing appearance and nice manners have failed to soften them. But I am full of bright and ingenious ideas. If this dagger or pin was bought in Bond Street, there are only two places likely to have sold it. Takurami's and Araby's. They are the only two who deal in Oriental curios. On the principle of finessing at Bridge — assume the cards will be where you want them to be — I'm assuming that it came from Araby's. The old man's a friend of mine, and when an Oriental is your friend — he *is* your friend. He'll help me all he can, I know."

"That seems an excellent idea," said Beryl, coolly. "Did you — er — ring up to chat about it?"

"I rang up," said Oliver, "to suggest that we lunch together. Valuable information from Bond Street is the bait to lure you with. Are you lured?"

They agreed to meet at a restaurant well known to both of them.

Araby's establishment was situated at the Piccadilly end of Bond Street. A sinuous young attendant slid forward as Oliver entered. Oliver demanded to see the proprietor. A few minutes later, he was following a tall dignified figure in a frock coat into the dimmer recesses of the shop.

Mr. Araby waved his guest to a chair and offered him a cigarette. He sat down, too. For some
minutes there was silence, the silence of the East,
where it is bad manners to rush into conversation
too soon. But hypnotised as he was by the atmosphere, Oliver made a determined effort to
"get on with it" in Western style.

"I mustn't take up too much of your time," he
began.

Mr. Araby waved time aside. He was, apparently, quite willing to sit there smoking all day.

"I want you to help me, if you will," said
Oliver.

"My help is ever at your service," said the
other courteously.

"It's this Lonely Bungalow Murder," said
Oliver. "They found the weapon at Victoria Station yesterday evening. It was bought here, was
it not?"

Araby inclined a dignified head.

"That is so. The Inspector from Scotland Yard
— he has been here. I have told him all I know."

"Can you describe the thing?"

"Properly speaking, it was a pin, not a dagger.
A long metal pin with a head of jade — green jade
— very handsomely carved — a design of delicately
interlaced fish — representing a River god."

"I suppose the thing is pretty well unique?"
asked Oliver.

"In this country, perhaps. There is no great
demand for them, but they are common enough
in the province from which they come. The
women wear them pinned through their hair —
two as a rule — the River god to ensure fertility

and long life and the Snake goddess representing immortality."

"The River god does not seem to have been working this time," remarked Oliver. "Perhaps he had been insulted, or something."

He wrote in his little notebook "Curse of the River god" and looked at it approvingly. He knew that there was an enormous credulous section of the public who delighted in occult love and mysterious Eastern curses.

"The fashions of the East become the fashions of the West," said Araby. "It was to pin a woman's hair that I sold the thing."

"How do you know that?" asked Oliver sharply.

"The gentleman who bought it told me so. He made a joke about long hair coming in again and how women were always anxious to wear the most barbaric ornaments if there was any excuse for doing so."

"What was the gentleman like?" asked Oliver.

"He was a stout gentleman with a waxed moustache. A member of the firm of Fisher and Flensburger of Brighton. He gave me their card and asked for trade discount."

"That is odd," said Oliver. Somehow he had not expected this open method of purchase. "And this was – when?" he asked.

"Last Friday afternoon about five o'clock."

"Friday afternoon," murmured Oliver. "The day before the murder at the Jumbles."

He sat thinking a minute or two longer. Then he rose to his feet. Mr. Araby, calm, incurious, and unaffected by any emotion, rose also.

"I'm extremely grateful to you," said Oliver.

"It is nothing," Araby waved the service aside.

"I suppose —" Oliver hesitated. "There is no question that the murders *were* committed with this pin?"

"The inspector seemed to have no doubt," said Araby. "The pin, you see, was not round but triangular, and also it had a little kink — so. I know something of surgery, my friend. A doctor would not be likely to make any mistake. The wounds would be quite distinctive."

Half an hour later, Oliver and Beryl were seated together at a small table.

"Well?" said Beryl eagerly, after the waiter had taken their order and moved away. "What about it? Have you been successful?"

Oliver nodded.

"It was Araby's all right."

"How splendid." Beryl was flushed with enthusiasm. "You know — I have been half afraid — the line was so bad that night — I could hardly hear what Mr. Johnson said. At first I thought it was Broad Street. It would be too dreadful if we had made a blunder."

"I always think," said Oliver, "that a woman should be interested heart and soul in her husband's work. You are a journalist to the core, Beryl. I feel that augurs well for our future."

"What are you talking about?" said Beryl.

"Marriage," said Oliver.

"Well, let us talk about something more interesting."

Oliver recounted his interview with the curio-dealer in full.

"You see," he said, as he ended, "it seems rather to put the lid on things. How Fisher wangled his alibi I don't know, but Fisher is evidently the man."

"He bought the pin on Friday and the girl was killed on Saturday. Yes, that does seem pretty conclusive," said Beryl.

"But giving his trade card and asking for discount — that seems the act of a lunatic."

Beryl disagreed.

"No — it only shows the crime wasn't premeditated. He bought the pin as a present, took it down to her, they had a quarrel and he stabbed her with it."

"Ye — es," allowed Oliver. "That's all right — and yet," he added, "it isn't."

"What do you mean — it isn't?"

"It's all right in theory — but it's all wrong for Fisher. Fisher isn't that kind of man. You're up against human nature."

"Yes," said Beryl slowly. "But isn't there always another side to people — a side you don't see?"

"The hidden self? Yes, perhaps you're right. The chained tiger."

His face altered for a moment or two, and he stabbed at his bread with his fork.

"There's the alibi, though," said Oliver. "And we know both murders were done by the same person."

"Yes, but do we?" said Beryl. "Supposing, for the sake of argument, that somebody wanted to kill Mr. Johnson. They may have wanted to for some time. Well, suddenly they get their chance. Johnson is coming up to town and he has with him the weapon with which a murder has already been committed. If he's found killed with that same weapon – what will everybody say? Why, that he's been killed by the original murderer, of course."

"Whilst really," said Oliver, "the two crimes are completely unconnected. By the way, there's one very strong point in Fisher's favour that nobody seems to have thought of."

"What's that?"

"Just this. Johnson had the weapon, didn't he? Well, if Fisher followed him up from Brighton – how did he get the weapon from Johnson in order to stab him with it?"

"That's a very good point," said Beryl warmly.

"Johnson wouldn't go handing over his precious find to a total stranger, and they can't have had a struggle at Victoria Station. Johnson must have been stabbed when he was completely unsuspicious."

"As he would be if it were someone he knew," Beryl pointed out.

"Yes," said Oliver. "But then nobody knew that he was coming up by the train except the people in the *Morning Star* office. As a matter of fact, the police have taken a statement from all of us as to our movements. But you know that."

"No, I didn't know."

"Well, they did, as a matter of routine. Still, that's not the real flaw. The real flaw is –"

He paused and looked questioningly at Beryl.

"I know," she said, nodding her head. "The real objection to my theory is that nobody could possibly want to murder Mr. Johnson. There's no earthly motive."

"Now if it had been the other way about," said Oliver. "Johnson *had* a motive for murdering me.

The successful rival."

"You really are the most conceited man," said Beryl coldly.

"And you are quite the most elusive woman. Talking of women, you know it ought to have been a woman who murdered Johnson."

"Why a woman?" Beryl's voice showed surprise.

"Because it would fit rather well. Stabbed in the back is a typical womanly crime – and the jade-headed pin is a typical woman's weapon. Think of it – the woman and Johnson by the telephone-cabinet – he shows her the jade pin – she takes it in her hand exclaiming at his cleverness. The poor unsuspecting devil turns his back on her and takes off the receiver and she jabs him one. I can almost see it happening. Johnson is just the kind of chap who would trust a woman blindly."

"Only there isn't any woman," said Beryl, cutting short his flight of fancy ruthlessly.

Oliver sighed.

"As you say, there is no woman." He looked at his watch. "I must be off. Let's just run over the case as it stands. Theory I: Fisher committed both murders, having chummed up to Johnson in the train and asked to see what was in the pretty parcel he was carrying. Or he might have pinched it out of Johnson's attaché case if Johnson were out of the carriage."

He paused and jabbed the table with a vicious finger.

"Theory 2: Fisher committed the first murder and an unknown enemy of Johnson's committed the second. Put out of court because we can't believe that Johnson had an unknown enemy. Theory 3: Tracey —"

"That's your theory," said Beryl. "You always want it to be Tracey."

"Well, why shouldn't it be? The absence of Mr. Tracey is so very definite. All England's looking for him — and finding him, worse luck! He really seems to be that mythical being — the average man. And yet, knowing himself to be hunted, I'd like to bet that sooner or later he gives himself away. That is unless —"

"Unless what?"

"Unless he's dead," said Oliver gravely.

"There was a momentary silence. Then Oliver went on in a lighter tone. "And that ends our list of suspects."

"No," said Beryl. "There's that man Potts."

"A nasty customer," said Oliver. "But I don't really see how he comes in."

"Unless," the colour flooded her face, "*Unless — Tracey is Potts.*"

"But, my dear, the scar —"

"You can fake a scar. I feel I'm right. Potts is Tracey. He came back to the bungalow because he'd left something behind — something incriminating. When you challenged him, he's startled, but he's got his story pat. He's heard mention of a brother at the inquest. So he boldly claims to be that brother."

"You forget I rang up Southampton and verified his story."

"That could be fixed. He may really *be* Potts. They may just have taken the name of Tracey for going down to the bungalow."

"But why should they take a bungalow in the name of Tracey?" asked Oliver. He was becoming fascinated by the theory, but in duty bound he continued to point out all the objections.

"I don't know," admitted Beryl, frankly.

"There might have been some shady reason," debated Oliver. "Something connected with blackmail, perhaps. Fisher might be involved in that."

He rose.

"I must be off. I'll bear this idea of yours in mind, Beryl. Are you coming?"

"I'll sit here a few minutes longer," said Beryl, consulting her wrist watch. "I don't have to get back for another ten minutes, and I'd like to think this thing out."

Oliver nodded, and catching up his overcoat and his dilapidated hat, he swung out of the restaurant. There was the sharp rustle of a newspaper from the next table as he passed.

It was so pronounced that it caught Beryl's attention. The table next to theirs was occupied by a solitary man sitting with his back to them. He was holding his newspaper now at a very curious sideways angle, and was seemingly absorbed in it. Beryl realised that, held at such an angle, the newspaper concealed his face from anyone passing him on the way out.

A sudden curiosity stirred in her. She got up, as though to leave, then moved round the table peering on the ground as though looking for a lost glove. In so doing, she reached a vantage point quite unsuspected by the occupant of the next table. From where she stood she could quite plainly see his face reflected in a mirror on the wall.

Secure, as he thought, behind his newspaper, the man was gazing towards the exit through which Oliver had just passed. The expression on his face was a curious one – an unpleasant kind of gloating triumph – yet with it a trace at least of some other feeling – fear, Beryl believed it to be. He was a dark, clean-shaven man of middle age, and down his right cheek there ran an ugly diagonal scar.

Potts! She was sure of it!

She waited until he paid his bill and left. Then, at a discreet distance, she followed. She had very little fear of his detecting her. If, as she believed, he had followed her and Oliver into the restaurant and deliberately tried to overhear their conversation, he had probably paid little attention to the girl with whom the reporter was talking.

Outside Holborn tube station the man paused. A crowd of people were coming out of the exit. Beryl saw a flash of white paper as he apparently passed something to one of them. She was not absolutely sure of this; she felt she might conceivably have been mistaken. But presently, the man having crossed over, the same process was repeated at the British Museum Station.

Again the man strolled on. At Tottenham Court Road Beryl had drawn abreast, suspecting that the same manoeuvre was going to be executed. This time there was no doubt. She saw the flash of white paper distinctly. The person who received it was a well-dressed woman, very much made up. She did not look at the paper in her hand, but went up to the booking office. Potts did the same, and Beryl followed suit. Beryl was unable to hear what station Potts booked to, but she herself took a fourpenny ticket to cover emergencies.

On the Hampstead platform all three waited for the train. The platform was crowded. The train buzzed in. Potts sprang aboard. As it came to the strange woman's turn to enter the train, the paper she was holding fell unnoticed to the ground. Quick as a flash Beryl bent and picked it up. By doing so she missed her chance of entering the train. The doors closed in her face.

She stood with the paper in her hand, and as the train passed slowly by her, she saw Potts's eyes fixed on her and on the paper she held. A malicious grin distorted his face.

Eagerly Beryl looked at her find and experienced a sharp pang of disappointment. It was a printed leaflet, and it ran:

GETTING RELIGION IS BETTER THAN
GETTING A JOB.
ARE YOU SAVED?

V

TRACING TRACEY

by anthony berkeley

Lord Ludgate thumped the table with a large fist. "We've got to find this fellow Tracey before the police do," he said.

His editor, his news-editor, and his crime-reporter nodded solemn agreement. It was to attend this important conference that Oliver had had to cut short his lunch with Beryl.

"Hang it all," Lord Ludgate growled, "one of our own men done in like that. . . . I'll double the reward!"

The editor, a laconic man, merely nodded. Hemingway said: "I doubt if that will really help." Oliver said nothing.

The *Morning Star*, foaming in every headline, had already offered five hundred pounds reward for information that would lead to the discovery of Tracey. Amid a spate of letters a few drops of real information had been thrown up. Between half a dozen different persons Tracey's normal movements on Monday mornings had been traced from the Jumbles to Brighton, from Brighton to Victoria, and thence into the Underground Railway and an eastward-bound train as far as Charing Cross. There the last of the informants had dropped out and Tracey was left in the train, still travelling east. Not the most hysterical endeavours of the *Morning Star* had been able to follow him further.

The significant point to Oliver in this journey was the fact that the train Tracey used to catch at Brighton was the 9:40, getting to Victoria at 10:59. It would therefore be well past eleven by the time he was at Charing Cross, and considerably later before he reached his destination. If he was bound for a business in the City, as seemed most probable, the inference was interesting: he must be in a big position. Only the boss can afford to arrive at work at that hour.

Oliver put this theory to the conference now.

"It may be a pointer," Lord Ludgate agreed. "Anyhow, try it. Try anything. I'm determined to get the brute who killed Johnson."

"And you still think that's Tracey?" said Hemingway, who had already put forward his own conviction that it was Fisher.

"We mustn't forget," interposed the editor, smoothly, "the suggestion that the murders may after all be unconnected."

"I've thought about that," said Lord Ludgate, briefly. "Nothing in it. If that was the case, don't you see the inference? Besides the Jumbles end, the only people who knew Johnson was coming up by that train were people in this office. I don't think we need consider that further. In any case, Johnson was popular, wasn't he? Nice young fellow? No enemies? Or didn't I once hear something about a row between him and one of the others?"

"Oh, you mean Redman? Yes, there was a little coolness once; about a girl, I believe; nothing serious." The tinkling of the telephone bell interrupted him. The editor attended to the instrument. "I see," he said, finally, after listening intently. "Thank you, Graves." He hung up the receiver. "The police have brought Fisher up from Brighton. They're taking him to Scotland Yard. He doesn't seem to be under arrest, but something's up."

"It'll be about the weapon," said Oliver. "I'd better get down there." In a few words he gave them the result of his interview with Araby that morning. Hemingway nodded towards Lord Ludgate, as if to say, "Fisher! I told you so."

On the way down to Scotland Yard Oliver decided that there could be only one possible reason for the police bringing Fisher up to London: to have him identified by Araby as the purchaser of the pin. This would mean, probably, that Fisher had denied the purchase. The possibilities looked interesting.

It was, however, some considerable time before Oliver could satisfy his curiosity. By careful enquiry he found out that an identification parade was certainly in progress, which confirmed his theory. It was absolutely essential that he should hear the result.

While he was still deliberating how to bring this about, an agitated little man fled out from the entrance to the building, with an umbrella in one hand and a bowler hat in the other, both of which he was waving at an expostulatory constable in his wake. Seeing the sergeant with whom Oliver was talking, he made a bee-line towards him, exclaiming: "I really cannot wait any longer. You must understand my time is valuable. I have my rights as a citizen. You must find somebody else to take my place in this parade. I'm in a great hurry."

Before the sergeant could reply, Oliver had stepped forward and answered for him: "Of course, sir. I quite agree. It's scandalous. I entirely identify myself with your protest, and I'll take your place with pleasure." He nudged the sergeant gently in the ribs and winked heavily.

The sergeant hesitated, and then gave permission and the little man scuttled off, flourishing his umbrella in triumph. When Fisher had been identified by Araby, to his intense disgust, Oliver found himself hustled with the others out of the room and out of the building. He wondered if Fisher had been arrested after all. He could get no information on that point, and was compelled to wait about, and go on waiting about.

At last, after nearly two hours, Fisher himself came out, unescorted. Oliver fastened on him like a dog on a bone. Fisher, glad, apparently, to see a friendly face, was quite ready to be led to the nearest house of liquid refreshment. Nor had Oliver the least difficulty in getting his story. Fisher, changing gradually from a badly frightened man to one not ill-pleased with himself, almost pressed it on him.

He *had* denied at first the purchase of the pin. It was foolish. He saw that now. But having in a moment of alarm taken that line, he had felt him-

self compelled to stick to it. Naturally this had
made the police suspicious. Quite naturally. But
now that Fisher had, in a frank and manly way,
admitted the purchase and explained, they were
quite satisfied.

Oliver nodded with apparent sympathy. He
saw plainly that Fisher, in insisting upon the
complete satisfaction of the police, was doing so
in order as much as anything to convince himself;
he was hoping that the police *were* satisfied. As
the story proceeded, Oliver himself was not so
sure.

Briefly, Fisher explained that the police, with
unpleasant cunning, had suddenly confronted
him that morning, in his own office, with a blood-
stained, jade-headed pin, and asked him if he had
ever seen it before. It was the first intimation
Fisher had had of the nature of the weapon: he
had asked, indeed, if it was the weapon. "Never
mind that," the police had replied sternly. "Have
you seen it before?" And Fisher, looking at that
darkly ominous blood, had lost his head for the
instant and replied that he had not. To the suggestion that the purchaser had tendered his own
trade-card, Fisher had pointed out (and the police
had been compelled to agree) that anyone might
have done that.

After he had then admitted, following his identification by Araby, that he had been the purchaser, the police had tried to trip him up again
by suggesting that he had taken the pin down
with him to the Jumbles on Saturday night; but
once again Fisher had been too many for them.
He had certainly not taken it with him; he had

posted it on the Friday. That this definitely linked the pin with Mrs. Tracey had seemed to please the police, but it could not hurt Fisher; and why? Because he had not only posted it, but had registered it, and had the counterfoil to prove it, which the police again had been bound to accept. They had asked him then when he saw the dagger again, after posting it, as if taking for granted that he had seen it again, but Fisher, never having seen it again, told them so straight. They had then been compelled, defeated at every turn, to let him go.

Oliver knew very well that the police could have been by no means satisfied, but had let Fisher go because there was simply no definite evidence on which he could be held; but that he was being kept under observation was as sure as that eggs make omelettes. The possibilities were obvious, but they remained as yet only possibilities: that the registered parcel, for instance, had contained something quite different; that Fisher did send the dagger, but picked it up at the Jumbles and committed murder with it; that Fisher saw the dagger in Geraldine Tracey's body when he called at nine that night and removed it, to hide it in the tree where Johnson had afterwards found it; and so on and so forth. Oliver did not, however, say a word about any such points. He merely pumped Fisher as dry of information as an out-of-date Bradshaw, and then left him.

Glancing at his watch as he emerged into the street, he saw that it was ten minutes to six. The time was propitious for another call he wanted to make before getting back to the office to write up his story.

Evanalda's was neither in Hanover Square, in Hanover Street, nor in Hanover Court. It was just off all of them. The time was past six o'clock when Oliver arrived there, and he was able to intercept the girl whose acquaintance he had already carefully made, just as she was leaving.

Oliver knew how to suit his methods to his individuals. If cream cakes and sundaes had been suitable for Gladys Sharp, cocktails at the Piccadilly Palace were indicated for Miss Amethyst Mainwaring.

Miss Mainwaring, a tall, intensely blonde young woman, besides being Evanalda's star mannequin, was on her own admission Geraldine Potts's best friend at Evanalda's. After a few introductory remarks upon Monte Carlo, the recent flat racing season, and the comparative merits of John Galsworthy and A. S. M. Hutchinson, which Oliver suffered because he knew she was determined to get them off her chest, Miss Mainwaring consented to tell what she knew about Tracey.

Unfortunately it seemed that her information did not amount to much more than was known already. Geraldine (said Miss Mainwaring) had spoken to her freely about Tracey, but not knowing much herself had not been able to supply many facts. The fiction of marriage had been maintained between the two girls, and never by so much as a hint had Geraldine suggested that such a ceremony was not to take place; but Miss Mainwaring had not been deceived.

"For I ask you, Mr. Oliver," she said, nibbling a salted almond with extreme delicacy, "I ask you, would Geraldine have been married and not invited *me*?" Well, I mean, I ask you."

"It stands to reason," Oliver agreed.

In the same way, Miss Mainwaring stated, the fiction had been upheld that Tracey was a commercial traveller. Even Geraldine had wavered on that point, to the extent of explaining that he must be a most superior commercial traveller, a kind of super-traveller, a traveller in battleships, or blocks of flats, or something equally stupendous. But again Miss Mainwaring had not been deceived. She knew, just *knew*, that Tracey was no commercial traveller; and she knew that Geraldine knew it too. "Why," said Miss Mainwaring, "he was quite the gentleman. Geraldine always said that."

"Then what do you think he was?" asked Oliver humbly. "In the City? A stockbroker, or something like that?"

But Miss Mainwaring did not think he was a stockbroker. He did not look like a stockbroker.

"How do you know what he looked like?" Oliver asked, not so humbly.

"Because I saw him, of course," replied Miss Mainwaring. "Geraldine pointed him out to me. Outside the Law Courts, in the Strand, it was. He was talking to another gentleman. Geraldine was going to meet him, at Charing Cross, but we saw him from the top of our bus outside the Law Courts."

Oliver concealed his excitement. "You saw him? I never knew that. Can you describe him? Would you recognise him if you saw him again?"

Miss Mainwaring was not sure. It had only been a glimpse, as you might say. He looked young – well, youngish, but, of course, that might have been the distance; quite ordinary, so to speak; fair perhaps rather than dark, but it was hard to say, him wearing a hat.

Oliver recognised that this description, vague as it was, differed from that supplied by other eyewitnesses of Tracey, but there might be reason for that. He thought rapidly. "And the man he was talking to? Can you describe him?"

Miss Mainwaring uttered a ladylike little snigger. "Well, there's such a lot to describe in a back, isn't there? Really, it might have been yours as well as anybody's for all I can say, Mr. Oliver."

"And leaving my back out of it, you can't put it any closer than that?" Oliver asked.

Miss Mainwaring could not.

Oliver was thoughtful as he left her twenty minutes later. He had decided to keep secret what he had learned. Miss Mainwaring's information was useless at present, but it might become exceedingly useful later on, and she with it. Better keep any such possibility in his own hands by not divulging it prematurely.

Oliver jumped on a 'bus that would carry him to Fleet Street, and mounted to the top. With one of the coincidences that happen more often on 'buses than anywhere else, he found himself sharing a seat with Beryl's fellow-secretary, Miss Timmins. Miss Timmins engaged him immediately in conversation. She had theories, it seemed, which she thought it only right that Oliver should learn.

"Fire 'em out, then," said Oliver, amused. "Decided who the murderer is, Miss Timmins?"

"Oh, yes," said Miss Timmins promptly. "I mean, surely that's quite plain, isn't it? I mean, it must be that man Potts."

"Oh!" said Oliver, with more interest, and remembering Beryl's own remarks on that subject. "Her own brother, eh?"

"Well, really, Mr. Oliver," said Miss Timmins, "you don't believe that, do you? You don't really believe he's her brother?"

"What do you think he is, then?" Oliver smiled.

"Her husband!" replied Miss Timmins promptly. "Oh, you needn't smile, Mr. Oliver. I'm quite, quite sure. Well, I mean, it stands to reason, doesn't it? He was her husband, and he's killed his wife and her lover. I mean, it stands to reason."

"Humph!" said Oliver, but he felt decidedly more respect for the little creature at his side. The theory was a plausible one, and certainly there was no evidence against it.

"I do think it's so unfair, the reward about finding Tracey not being open to members of the staff," Miss Timmins was lamenting.

"Oho! So you think you know where Tracey is too, do you?" Oliver asked.

"*Who* he is," Miss Timmins corrected, "because of course he isn't himself. I mean, he isn't really Tracey."

"Well, who is he?"

"It was something I said to Miss Blackwood once that gave me the idea," Miss Timmins answered modestly. "I said: 'And mark my words, dear' — I always call Beryl 'dear'; I *do* think she's such a nice girl, don't you, Mr. Oliver? — 'Mark my words, dear,' I said, 'the murderer's done in Mrs. Tracey, and what's more he's done in Tracey too. That's why they can't find Tracey. He's been done in.' And -- well, poor Mr. Johnson *was* murdered, wasn't he?"

"Miss Timmins," said Oliver in astonishment, "What exactly are you suggesting?"

"Why," said Miss Timmins, in surprise at such density. "Why, that Mr. Johnson was Tracey, of course. I mean, it stands to reason."

VI

SCOTLAND YARD ON THE JOB

by freeman wills crofts

While the *Morning Star* continued noisily running the Jumbles case for all it was worth, Scotland Yard was equally busy. Chief Inspector Bradford was in charge, and now sat in his room, presiding over a conference.

"We'll have a general run over things," he was saying, "but what I want particularly to do at this meeting is to bring our list of suspects up to date. We know the general situation. This man Tracey brings the girl down to the bungalow at the Jumbles. Then when Tracey's back is turned this other man Fisher comes butting in. The girl tries to run them both at the same time; a dangerous situation. Well, the girl gets done in and Inspector Smallpiece goes down to investigate. Now, Smallpiece, get along and tell us what you did."

"I went out to the bungalow and had a look round," Smallpiece began. "It's a small, four-roomed hut, hidden in a valley of the South

Downs; a very deserted, lonely spot. Enough to give the girl the hump in a week. Next I went round and had a chat with anyone I could find, the servant, the nearest neighbours, the tradesmen and so on. From these enquiries I got my first bit of information. Tracey was seen coming from the bungalow about half past seven on the evening of the murder."

"The devil he was!" the chief exclaimed. "That's news to me. Who saw him?"

"The conductor of a 'bus from Newhaven to Brighton," Smallpiece returned. "This man has a sweetheart living in the lane that leads past the Jumbles, and it was through her I got on to him. There was some little talk in the district about the Traceys, and the girl pointed out Tracey to the conductor. The conductor recognised Tracey at once. He got in near the end of the Jumbles lane and got out at Brighton."

"About seven-thirty?" the chief repeated. "And the murder was committed between seven and nine-thirty. That's a pity. It still leaves it open."

"It still leaves it very much open, sir, for Fisher's car was seen turning into the lane about nine o'clock."

"Yes, that's what he told the Brighton men. What it amounts to then is this: both Tracey and Fisher could have committed the crime. But we can't prove either did, and for all we know to the contrary, fifty other people might have been there."

"Smallpiece didn't think that likely. In his opinion Tracey was their man."

"Why so, Smallpiece?" asked the chief.

"Here, sir, you have Tracey bringing this girl down to the bungalow, and she's no sooner settled than she starts in with Fisher. Well, what's going to happen when Tracey finds that out? Suppose on that Saturday Tracey sees this pin Fisher gave her and asks her where she got it. Then the fat's in the fire. Tracey finds she's as false as sin. He seizes the pin and sticks her with it."

"That's right enough, but it's nearly as good put the other way round. Fisher takes her on provided she gives Tracey the go-by. She says she will; then she says she has. Then Fisher comes in and finds, let us suppose, Tracey's gloves. So Fisher learns she's as false as sin and he does her in. Not so likely, Smallpiece, but possible, and we can't overlook it."

Smallpiece admitted that that was so.

"Then," went on the chief, "what about this Potts? That's the man that confounded newspaper fellow, Oliver, started the hare about."

Smallpiece permitted a certain indignation to creep into his manner.

"He thought he'd done the big fellow over that, Oliver did. He'd got exclusive information for the *Morning Star*. And he wouldn't so far demean himself as to give the police the tip, not he. He found the man trying to break into the bungalow, and a nice mess he made of it. If he'd had the wit of a chimpanzee he'd have let the man get in, found out what he was after, and taken him as he was coming out. And then to let him get clear away! It fairly gets my goat when I think of a chance like that being lost."

"Yes," the chief agreed, "we owe the *Morning Star* a good deal over this case. Who is on to Potts?

Oh, you, Tinsley. Got anything?"

A tall thin man awoke to life.

"I think Potts is okay, sir," he answered, "but I've not been able to prove it yet. Potts told Oliver he was a steward on the Southampton – le Havre boat. There is a steward of that name but till I get him face to face with Oliver I can't be sure he's the same man. As to what he was after, I don't know, but if you remember, it was mentioned at the inquest that the girl had a brother, though she had seen nothing of him for a long time. I am making inquiries, and probably this will turn out to be the missing man."

The chief nodded. "Put it beyond doubt," he directed. "In the meantime I'll hold Potts on my list of suspects. Now, Smallpiece, will you finish what you have to tell us."

"I got some further information through the 'bus conductor, sir. He remembered Tracey having gone into Brighton with him one Monday morning. I went by the same bus on the following Monday, and had a chat in turn with the regular travellers. At last I found a man who had gone with Tracey up to town. It happened that they had then both got into the same Inner Circle train at Victoria. The man got out at Charing Cross, but Tracey went on in the train. So there, sir, we've found that he works somewhere east of Charing Cross."

"Good, Smallpiece," the chief approved. "Anything more from the Jumbles end?" He paused, looking round, then resumed: "Now with regard to the Victoria crime. Here, I take it, the question is: Who knew that Johnson had discovered something vital and was going to town by the 8:35 train?"

There were murmurs of approval and the chief went on: "Let us begin with our three Jumbles suspects. Could Tracey or Fisher or Potts have known?"

"Easily, sir," Smallpiece answered. "It might happen like this. The murderer, being upset after the crime, loses his head and puts the weapon into that hollow tree, about as darned silly a place as he could have well found. He tumbles to this afterwards, so he goes back to get it. As luck would have it he is just in time to see Johnson find it. Well, what can he do? He follows Johnson, intending to do him in, but till he gets to Victoria he cannot find an opportunity."

"Yes, that is possible enough," the chief approved. "Very good, suppose that happened. Now so far as we know, either Tracey or Potts might have done that. But could Fisher? Fisher had an alibi for the Victoria crime."

"I went into that, sir," spoke up another voice. "The man had an alibi, but it was just not quite watertight. At the same time I think he is innocent."

"Let's have the details."

"First of all, there was no one about Fisher's shop between the time the staff left and the charwoman came on duty, and in that time Fisher could have gone out to the Jumbles and seen Johnson find the weapon. Then about that dinner. If Fisher had been making a fake he could have pushed that dinner into a can and been out of the building in five minutes. He says the char was working at the front door, and so she was; but there is a back door he conveniently did not mention. He could have caught the 8:35, committed the murder at Victoria, and returned by the 11:05 to Brighton. Then he could have gone to the office, put out the light and got his hat and coat. Remember, sir, he did not get home till 12:30."

The chief nodded without speaking.

"Besides that, sir," went on the inspector, "if Fisher was not faking an alibi, why didn't he dine in the hotel? It was just across the road. And then there is his not reporting the murder for three hours after he admits he discovered it, and all his lies and shuffling about buying the pin."

"Then why do you think he is innocent?"

"For three reasons, sir. First there is his personality. Fisher does not seem to be the sort of man to commit murder. Second, he is well known at Brighton, and he was not seen at the station. Third, his story about the new partner turning up next day was true. Of course I know that none of these points is conclusive."

The chief grunted. "We'll hold Fisher on our list," he declared. "Now there are still all those newspaper people. Who was looking into the London end? You, Smart? Very well, get along and tell us about it."

Smart was a man whose name fitted his personality. He was looked upon as one of those competent officers in the force.

"I began, sir, by fixing the time of the murder. As you know, Johnson was just in the act of making a call when he was stabbed. He had lifted off the receiver, but had not given the number. I went round to the exchange and found that the call had been made at ten-four, that is, four minutes after the train got in.

"I next searched the telephone-box, but besides finding the weapon on the top, which you know about, I could only get one clue. The murderer had hung up an OUT OF ORDER notice, evidently to prevent people going in and finding the body. This notice was on cardboard, cut from a larger sheet, and the words OUT OF ORDER were roughly printed in blue pencil. Unfortunately the cardboard was too rough to show fingerprints."

"That's all very interesting, Smart," the chief commented, "but don't let's get away from what we're on to – who of those newspaper people knew that Johnson was travelling by that train?"

"Yes, sir. Well, I may say that there were quite a lot of people knew about Johnson coming up to town that night. First of all, Hemingway, the day news-editor, knew it, for he took Johnson's message. Redman, the night editor, knew it, for he was told it when he came in at seven-thirty. The chief sub-editor knew it. In fact, at least a dozen of the staff knew it, our friend Oliver among the number."

The chief shrugged. "It wouldn't matter who knew it," he said, "so long as no one left the building."

"That was my next job, sir; to find out if any of this lot had left the building. There were four. There were Hemingway and Redman, the day and night editors, Reporter Oliver and a second reporter called Peters. Next I asked these four where they were at ten o'clock, when the train came in. Two of them had alibis and two of them hadn't."

The men were showing close attention. Smart's reputation was standing him in good stead.

"Let's have the whole thing," the chief said. "Even if it led nowhere, let's hear what you did. Who had the alibis?"

"Hemingway and Reporter Peters."

"Well, take Hemingway. That was the day editor, to whom Johnson spoke. What was his alibi?"

"Hemingway called at his club that evening, sir, and went home to his house in Hampstead about ten. The thing from my point of view hinged on the actual time he got home. I was able to prove that it was not later than ten minutes past ten. The murder was committed at four minutes past ten. Now, it would be physically impossible for anyone to get from that telephone-box at Victoria to Hampstead in six minutes."

"How did you prove he got in at ten-ten?"

"This way, sir. When he went home he turned on the wireless, and about five minutes later the ten-fifteen time signal came through."

"Very well," the chief agreed. "Pass Hemingway. Who's next? This Reporter Peters?"

"He went straight home from the office," Smart answered. "That's vouched for by his wife, his mother, two sisters and a friend who was paying a call."

"Good enough."

"In each case good enough for the Victoria affair, yes," Smart agreed. "But, sir, neither Hemingway nor Peters had an alibi for the Jumbles murder."

"If the same man committed both crimes, an

alibi for one of them is enough. Pass them both."

"The next, sir, is Oliver. That's their star crime reporter."

"The man who has given us so much trouble on this job," the chief interjected bitterly.

"That's the man, sir. Oliver had no alibi for the Victoria affair. He says he dined in his rooms and about nine o'clock went out for a walk. He didn't get back to the newspaper office till ten-twenty. So he could have done the Victoria job. On the other hand he had an alibi for the Jumbles business. He was working that Saturday in the office. That's all right, for it's substantiated by a dozen people."

The chief nodded. "Next," he said laconically.

"Next comes Redman, the night editor. So far as alibis go, he's the worst, for he has no alibi for either crime. He's a queer sort of man is Redman; not sour, he's pleasant enough, but he lives in a flat by himself and doesn't mix much with people. All the same it's hinted that a visit to a nice girl in a lonely bungalow wouldn't come amiss to the same man. And then again, his living alone in a flat leaves him free to be away for weekends without anyone being any the wiser."

"Anything to connect him with the crime?"

"Nothing, sir, except that there was bad blood between him and Johnson. I've not been able to get just what the trouble was. I'm still working on that."

The chief whistled thoughtfully and added another note to his list.

"Get it cleared up," he said. "We can't pass Redman under these conditions." He looked again over his notes. "That leaves us with four suspects: from the Jumbles end, Tracey, Fisher and Potts, and from the newspaper end, Redman. You, Smart, have eliminated all the rest?"

"I'm not so sure, sir," Smart said doubtfully. "I may admit that I've wondered about Oliver. You can make a pretty strong case for these crimes being separate and for Oliver having done the Victoria one. As you know, sir, he and Johnson were pretty badly gone on Beryl Blackwood, the manager's secretary. They were also rivals in their work and this scoop of Johnson's must have annoyed Oliver considerably. If Oliver had wanted to get rid of his rival he couldn't have had a better opportunity. And as I said, Oliver has no alibi."

The chief considered.

"Get it cleared up," he said. "You should do that easily enough. Now that adds a suspect. Five suspects. Five suspects," he repeated slowly, "but to my way of thinking, Fisher, Potts and Oliver are not so likely as the other two."

There were general murmurs of approval.

"If so," the chief went on, "that leaves us, provisionally, with Tracey and Redman." He paused, slowly rubbing his chin and looking round the assembly. "And, what's wrong," he went on impressively, "what's wrong with Tracey *being* Redman?"

VII

BERYL IN BROAD STREET

by clemence dane

At one o'clock on a foggy November Saturday, Miss Beryl Blackwood, very trim but rather tired, paused on the steps of the *Morning Star* offices to buy a bunch of violets from a husky flower-boy. Pinning the bunch on her coat to advertise the fact that her half-holiday had begun, she smiled at the over-paid flower-boy and marched off into the fog.

Not for nothing did Miss Beryl Blackwood of the *Morning Star* possess a pugnacious, tip-tilted, but thoroughly attractive nose. Not for nothing had one small crease established itself between her carefully plucked eyebrows. Not for nothing did her lips meet firmly over her large white teeth. Not for nothing had she a chin.

A weaker young woman would have had her mind made up for her by the impetuous Oliver or poor adoring Johnson within a fortnight. But Miss Blackwood had contrived to balance the scales of her affections pretty equally between these two personable young men till fate had dropped a Chinese jade-headed pin into one of the scales and down went the scale and there was an end of poor Johnson. Because he was gone and a little haloed by his tragedy, she thought of him tenderly and was the more critical of Oliver.

In spite of all Oliver chose to say or the police chose to say, she knew Johnson's voice and she could trust her own memory. Johnson had said Broad Street, not Bond Street. She didn't care whether the pin came from Bond Street or Timbuctoo, poor murdered Johnson had talked of Broad Street.

She was thinking these things to herself as she walked across Fleet Street. She made a point of walking home on her half-holiday, partly for exercise, and partly because in the by-streets she could pick up housewifely odds and ends: fruit and strange cheese, a smoked mackerel, some liver sausage or any other of the peculiar foods which the bachelor girl and the foreigner enjoy. She then saw, in a trusty little creamery, some pots of home-made marmalade. Unthinkingly, she bought three and found them heavy carrying. Next a couple of corn-cobs went into her attaché-case from the greengrocer's at the corner by the animal shop. Then she stood a long ten minutes watching the animals and worrying because they were all in cages and asking her to take them out. There was one puppy in particular, ingratiating, thin, with beseeching eyes that wanted her very badly. It looked at her exactly as poor Johnson used to look at her. She asked its price. A pound!

Out of the question. Poor puppy: poor Johnson!

The fog drew down thicker as she walked away
and depressed her nerves with its ghostly qui-
eting of all sound. But the fog outside her was
nothing to the fog of depression in her mind. It
had settled down on her after the death of poor,
lovesick Johnson, and she had a panicky feeling
that it would not lift again until she had done
something to ease that unwilling ghost. She felt
suddenly resentful of the office, of Hemingway,
even of Oliver, but most of all she resented the
great newspaper and its great public. All they
cared for, this newspaper that she served and this
vast public that she served, was the scoop; nobody cared for Johnson, provider of the grand
sensation. He was no more than the man in the
poem, butchered to make a reader's holiday – and
Johnson *had* said Broad Street, not Bond Street!
She grew more and more sure of it, and then her
thoughts strayed back to the beseeching puppy,
and then she began to wonder where she was.
The fog had pressed down so heavily that she had
long since lost her sense of direction. She thought
that if only a taxi would come by she would take
it and then thought that the taxi home would be
at least half-a-crown. And eight half-crowns
would buy the puppy! And again, thinking of the
beast with its asking eyes, the dead man came
into her mind and this time she could not drive
him out. Indeed, she did not try. She had a feeling
that the fog had come on purpose to shut her out
from the world of the living, to create a private
chamber in the heart of London. In it she and the
dead man, so terribly alive in her mind, were to

have their last interview.

She said to herself: "If I were a spiritualist now, I should say he were trying to get through to me." And then, on an impulse, stood stock still in the deserted street – she could not see a yard ahead of her – and said to the wall of fog: "All right. If he is anywhere and wants to tell me anything, let him try. I'm in the mood." And stood, superstitiously waiting for some sort of an answer to come to her out of the filthy quiet.

None came, of course. And after that moment's pause, she shrugged at her own folly and prepared to walk on again, only to realise that she had indeed lost her sense of direction completely. She peered upwards, but the fog was too thick for her to see the name of the street.

What was she to do? Her arm ached and she was wasting her precious holiday!

At that moment of her indecision a familiar footfall made itself heard, the comforting footfall of the London policeman, and six feet of most unghostly blue cloth loomed up out of the universal yellow. Beryl was thankful and showed it with a flash of white teeth.

"Officer, I've lost my way. D'you know where we are?"

"Broad Street, Miss."

"Broad Street!" She gave a little shiver. It was uncanny to have thought so intensely for the last quarter of an hour of a dead man and his last words and then to have these last words echoed, loudly, cheerfully, by the livest of live policemen. "Broad Street. . . ."

"Is there a curiosity shop in Broad Street, officer?"

"Yes, Miss. Farther along on the same side."

She thanked him and went on, curiously excited, saying to herself:

"Of course Oliver'll just say 'coincidence.' So it is coincidence if you look at it like that, but it's queer all the same. I ought to buy that puppy now, poor little beast, for bringing me luck! I can, if I economise on lunches for a fortnight. Broad Street. He *did* say Broad Street. Ah, here we are."

It was a mean little shop with a mean little door. It had the air of a shop doomed. "I shall be pulled down in five years," said the little shop, "so I am not taking any trouble about my paint."

Nevertheless, in its window was spread out just the sort of litter that attracts any junk-hunter: half a dozen bad miniatures, one good daguerreotype in a modern frame, some vile Bohemian glass, some dirty ivory brushes, a ten-shilling tray of trifles, and a pale yellow witchball.

"My sort of shop," said Beryl to herself: she was a born picker up of trifles. "And I'll have that witchball or die."

In she went. An old-fashioned tin bell jingled and through the bead curtains of an inner office the proprietress came out. Beryl had never been in the little shop before, but she knew the lady well, with her art jumper, her untidy, sketchily waved hair, her equally sketchy make-up, her avarice and her glib half-knowledge. But Beryl had a good way in a shop. Her air, her smile, her carriage, all said: "I haven't got much to spend, but I know what I want and I like you and I shan't waste your time."

She loosed the manner upon the lady of the shop and the lady of the shop responded by instantly beginning to waste Beryl's time. In the end, Beryl picked up a tea-caddy cigarette-box to give to Oliver, and was offered the really beautiful witchball at some two pounds less than its proper value. By this time they were so confidential, that Beryl felt it was time to get on the track of the Chinese pin. Behold her at the game!

"You see, I'd like the witchball for a wedding present," said Beryl. "But it's pure extravagance. I mean one's friends don't expect – when one's hard up –"

"Depends on your friends, dear," said the lady in the jumper. "But what I say is, when you get your chance take it. I shouldn't be offering it at that price if I hadn't got it cheap myself."

"It's the bother of sending," murmured Beryl. "You'd pack it for me, of course?"

"No. That I do not undertake," said the lady of the shop firmly. "Anything reasonable in the way of brown paper. . . ."

"I suppose you haven't anything else, that would be more packable – an ornament of some sort," said Beryl.

"Well what about the earrings – real Oriental topaz?"

"Her ears aren't pierced."

"Well, dear, it's only a question of having them fixed on screws."

"Could you get that done for me?" said Beryl hopefully.

"I'm sorry. No. If I had to go running about getting screwtops fixed on earrings – I mean it takes me all my time finding the stuff nowadays, let alone selling it. There was a customer in last month – took a fancy to a Chinese pin in the ten and sixpenny tray. 'Could you find me the pair?' he says. 'I could not,' I said. 'It's very unique, that pin is. If you want replicas you can go to Birmingham,' I said. 'There's nothing sold in this shop that isn't genuine *and* guaranteed.' 'No offence, I hope,' he says. 'None at all,' I said, 'unless it's offered. But that pin's unique.'"

"What sort of a pin?" said Beryl.

"Oh – one of those Oriental pins," said the lady vaguely. "How anyone could keep their hair up with it – more like a skewer than a pin! That's why I sold it cheap. With all this shingling," said the lady, patting her head complacently.

"It sounds the sort of thing that I'm looking for," said Beryl, controlling her excitement. "A hairpin you say?"

"Yes, dear. For the hair. Jade."

"How much was it?"

"Well, I charged him ten shillings," returned the lady of the antiques, pleased at her customer's regret, and not sorry to enhance it. "Cheap. Yes. It would have done you. Very artistic. A woman's head all over snakes. All carved."

Beryl started. Surely Oliver had described differently the deadly pin that stabbed poor Johnson. Chinese, yes. Jade, yes. But it had been a carved man's head on a fish's body. But if the dead Johnson had been right and the pin he had found, the pin which had undoubtedly stabbed the woman at the Jumbles, were bought at Broad Street, then the pin which had ended his own life was not the same weapon. On Johnson's pin had been a woman's head on a snake's. Alike, but not the same pin, then. One murderer – two pins? Two murderers – one pin? The dreadful arithmetic was beyond her. And at once she found her resentment against Oliver ebbing. He had such a quick tongue: he always knew what to do. She wished she had him at her side, but as she racked her brains for an excuse to ask the question that he would ask so easily, the woman of the shop, rambling on, saved her the trouble.

"I wouldn't worry, dear. After all," the ruler of the antiques was murmuring, "it needed repair. That's customers all over," she continued bitterly. "First they want a thing old as the hills and then they expect you to give it 'em as good as new. 'Of course, you'll put it in order,'" said the lady of the antiques, breaking out suddenly into a startling, but spirited, rendering of that proud-nosed, high-voiced monster, the female customer, and fixing, withal, a challenging eye upon Beryl. "'Of course, you'll have the hinge put on: of course, you'll get it riveted; of course, you'll 'ave it restrung!' Yes, my dear, a good hour they'll spend pricing every antique in the shop, and then they'll pick out a cairngorm brooch from the half-crown tray and expect me to put a pin on for 'em! You'd think I kept the shop to oblige them. If I've said it once," said the lady of the shop, passionately, "I say it once a day, I'm not repairs: I'm antique. I told him so when he bought the Chinese pin . . ."

"Oh, a man bought it?" said Beryl.

"I should think it was a man. Milord-own-the-earth, I should think! 'If you want it repaired,' I said, 'why don't you take it somewhere yourself? Where d'you take your spectacles when they're broken? Well, they'd do it for you.' For he was wearing horn-rimmed spectacles — But no, milord

couldn't be bothered, and sooner than lose a customer, I said, 'Oh, well, leave me your address
and I'll get it done. What name?' I says. 'Oh,' he
says, looking at me as if I'd asked him to explain
the Epstein theory – 'Oh, er,' he says, 'Dedham,'
he says, or 'Deadman,' or something, but before
I could write it down he goes and changes his
mind again. Says something about not troubling
me. Not troubling me, mark you! And then after
wasting twenty minutes of my valuable time, he
slams down a ten shilling note and walks out of
the shop. Men," said the lady of the antiques el-
oquently, "that's what I always say, *men*! But
there, one mustn't be hard. If you'll take my ad-
vice, dear, you'll stick to the witchball. It's
unique, that witchball is."

Beryl, gathering up her purchases, would not
commit herself about the witchball. But might
she come in again and see it? Any day between
twelve and one? Very well, and if Beryl wasn't
able to get away, her friend, whose name was
Oliver, would come in alone. And meantime, if
Mr. Deadham, Deadman, what was the name?
should want to change his purchase – people did
sometimes, didn't they? – Beryl would be very
glad to know. She left her name, address, and a
good impression behind her and walked out of
the little shop, her head in a whirl.

What had she learned? Anything? Nothing?
Who was the purchaser of the pin? The man in
horn spectacles who would not leave his address,
whose name haunted one because of its resem-
blance to Redman – Dedham, Deadman, Redman! This was a job for Oliver, not for her. And
she was thankful that she had asked Oliver to tea,

and that he would already be, as she knew, sitting at the door of her flat, waiting for her. Well, he could wait another quarter of an hour. She was not going to forget her luck-bringer.

She retraced her steps swiftly, for the fog was lightening in the sudden way a London fog will, till she reached the animal shop. There was the puppy, wanting her worse than ever. It was sheer madness to spend a pound on a shivering puppy, which probably had not had distemper. It would mean porridge, and glasses of milk at a bun shop, for an indefinite period. Beryl thought it out sensibly and quietly and then she went in and bought the puppy. And because the little beast, delirious with excitement, was difficult to hold, as well as the marmalade and the celery and the attaché case, Beryl crowned her follies by a taxi home.

She was perfectly right in her forecast. Oliver *was* sitting on the stairs. Oliver was cold: Oliver was cross: Oliver had been there, he was careful to tell her, a good seven minutes. Nevertheless, Oliver was pleased to be in the position of a patient martyr, and when she had apologised sufficiently, took the key from her in a masterful oh-you-women-come-along-give-it-to-me way that indicated forgiveness.

"I've bought a puppy," said Beryl rather breathlessly, and let the excited beast wriggle out of her coat.

"My dear Beryl, what on earth for? I loathe dogs," said Oliver. But he took it from her as he spoke, and handled it as dogs like to be handled. And the puppy was charmed and tried to attend to both of them at once and generally made it known that he liked them both. Then Beryl beamed at Oliver and Oliver beamed back and the puppy, suddenly finding itself disregarded, began to bark.

"Where did you get him?" said Oliver.

"A turning out of Broad Street," said Beryl slowly.

"Broad Street?" He looked at her blankly. Then: "What is it, Beryl?" he said. "You've been up to something. Out with it."

"If I told you," she said, "that Mr. Redman had bought a Chinese pin exactly like the pin that Johnson found at a shop in Broad Street, what would you say?"

"I shouldn't believe it," said he.

"But if I could prove it?" said she.

"*Redman*?" he asked, incredulously.

"Dedham is the actual name I got out of the woman. But it's pretty like Redman and the description's exact. You don't think, do you . . . ?"

The two stared at each other, while the puppy barked more furiously than ever.

VIII

THE SAD TRUTH ABOUT POTTS

by e. c. bentley

For some time after hearing Beryl Blackwood's story of the second pin and its purchaser, so strangely named Dedham or Deadman, Oliver turned the matter over in his mind with uneasiness. The notion of Redman being involved in some way with one or both of the crimes which he was investigating was a new idea altogether. Was it a very good one? The similarity of the name, as remembered by the woman of the Broad Street shop, was a striking fact taken in connection with the circumstance that her description of the purchaser fitted Redman well enough. But, thought Oliver, it would fit thousands of other men as well; such figures, with nothing at all remarkable about them, are the rule. As for the ridiculous name of Deadman, need it be supposed that Redman was the name she was trying to recollect? Why not Steadman? — a much commoner name. Why not Denman? Or Denham?

On the other hand, there had been that trouble between Redman and young Johnson. In the case of a queer, reserved fellow like Redman, who could say how deep that had gone? And he had, as Oliver knew, been able to give the police an account that could be tested of his movements after leaving the *Morning Star* on the evening of the Victoria Station crime.

But the truth was, as Oliver put it to himself plainly, that he had no idea at all of following up this Redman clue, if clue it could be called. He was on a friendly footing with the man; they were colleagues in a calling that sets the highest value on loyal team-work. Also, Oliver was not paid by the *Star* to follow up flimsy suspicions as to the conduct of another member of that journal's staff. If that had to be done, the police could attend to it for themselves.

A much more substantial job of work, in Oliver's sincere opinion, was put before him by the case of Arthur Potts. Beryl and Miss Timmins, between them, had most effectually reawakened his interest in that plausible steamboat steward. Oliver had never completely wiped Potts out of the picture of possibilities; but as he had told a straight story about himself and his movements, it had seemed better to follow up more promising lines of inquiry. Now, however, Potts most certainly demanded attention. There was the suggestion that the man seen by Oliver at the bungalow, who gave his name as Arthur Potts, brother of the victim, had simply assumed the identity of that same Potts. If that man had known the real Potts and his circumstances well enough, and had known about a steward's job, he could have

worked the deception up to a point. It must have
broken down, of course, if Oliver had followed
him to Southampton on the evening of their meeting, and had waited for the actual Potts going on
duty that night in the le Havre boat.

And if the so-called Potts had simply been
making his escape from an awkward situation? If
he had been, in fact, the missing Tracey?

Or if, again, Potts had been Potts in truth and
in fact and his account of himself an honest one,
with the material exception that, instead of being
the brother of the murdered woman, he had been
her husband? Oliver's opinion of the intelligence
of Miss Timmins had never been a high one; but
he felt obliged to admit that this shot of hers was
very far from being off the target. Potts married
to Geraldine, although for some unknown reason
living with her only at intervals; Potts discovering
himself to be an injured husband; Potts appearing
at the bungalow to accuse his wife, and finding
her preparing that very evening to welcome
Fisher, the usurper of his conjugal rights; Potts
mad with rage, Geraldine shrill in abuse and in-
sult; Potts a murderer; Potts, returning to Brighton on the day of the inquest, haunted by the fear
of having left some trace of his presence in the
bungalow, and driven to take the risk of attempt-
ing to enter the place and remove that evidence;
Oliver could see very well how it all fitted together.

But what, then, of the mysterious being in the
Holborn restaurant whom Beryl believed to have
been watching him, Oliver; who was scared like
Potts; and who had pursued such strange evan-
gelical activities? What was to be made of all that?

Clearly, thought Oliver, the first thing to be done was to seek out the real Potts at Southampton and test the first link of the chain. If the real Potts was a man Oliver had never seen, then there was little doubt that Oliver had let the murderer escape, and that would be the highly unfortunate and humiliating end of it. But if the real Potts turned out to be the man of the bungalow, then there would be a task of research-work indeed into the history and movements of that employee of the Southern Railway Company.

On the morning after his adventure at Scotland Yard and his interview with Evanalda's mannequin, Oliver put this new view of the case to Hemingway at the office, and found him ready to take a favourable view of it. "Mind you," he said, "with what we and the police have got now about Fisher and the buying of the dagger, there's less doubt than ever of his being the man. But Fisher can't get away; they've got him taped; and this notion of Potts being the husband is a heap too good to be turned down. If it's true, it'll make a whale of a story; and of course, Fisher may be the murderer just the same, even if there were a van-load of injured husbands scooting around to keep things lively. Go to it, Oliver."

In Southampton that afternoon Oliver began his inquiries at the company's office by the harbour. In the character of a prospective passenger to le Havre, he established the facts that the service was a nightly one; that the boats working it were due to leave, as the so-called Potts had said, at 11:15; that they were timed to arrive at 6:20 in the morning; that they started on the return journey to Southampton the same night at 11:30, ar-

riving at 6:30 a.m. A steward, then, would spend
alternate days in Southampton and le Havre, with
most of the day at his disposal for rest, recreation
or private business. In the unlikely event of a
servant of the company being on duty for as much
as ten hours, there was plenty of time, Oliver
thought uncharitably, for him to get into mischief
during the rest of the twenty-four. There was also
his weekly day off, whenever that might happen
to be. No more than any other trade unionist
would Potts be chained to his bench in the galley.

The abode of Potts, of which both the man at
the bungalow and the company had given Oliver
the address, turned out to be one of a street of
very small and for the most part decent houses
near the harbour. Its clean lace curtains and whi-
tened door-sill, the cage of canaries visible in one
window and the india-rubber plant in another,
spoke gently but firmly of respectability. Oliver
on this occasion was an old friend of Potts, anxious to renew their comradeship, and speaking
with a very creditable Yorkshire accent. He was
not surprised to hear that Potts was that day in le
Havre, and would not be at home until breakfast-
time the next day. The elderly woman who had
opened the door to Oliver was a sympathetic
soul, not indisposed to talk. Mr. Potts, she was
sure, would be glad to see him; Mr. Potts saw so
few gentlemen at the house. No, said the old
woman, Mr. Potts had not married during the few
years since Oliver had seen him last; he seemed
to feel himself quite comfortable as he was.

It scarcely needed the reporter's light hand on
the reins of the conversation to bring out the fact
that the housekeeper had been with Potts no

more than eighteen months; from which there was a natural and easy passage to the remark from Oliver that the place was kept so much better than it used to be, he hardly knew it. When this was followed by the brazen inquiry whether Potts still kept canaries, the fortress was won. Oliver was invited, without asking, to see the front parlour, and his attention was directed to recent improvements in its furnishing and decoration. Potts, remarked Oliver, had always been a saving man. More than that, the old woman said, Mr. Potts had come into a bit of money about a year ago; he had told her so. He could afford to give up his job, in her belief, whenever he liked, and live like a gentleman.

What was at least clear to Oliver was that Potts was living, privately and unobtrusively, in a style considerably beyond the means of a steamboat steward. He noticed particularly a wireless set which, to his knowledge, must have cost much more than the sum which the old woman, thinking to dazzle the visitor, guessed Potts must have paid for it; and the presence of a small safe in a corner of the room did not escape the reporter's observant eye.

Perhaps the best time, Oliver suggested, for him to call on Potts would be on his day off, when they might have a long evening together. That, the housekeeper said, was Saturday; but most often on the Saturdays Mr. Potts, after he had had his sleep, would pack his bag and go off-a-visiting somewhere, not coming back until the next day. He liked to see a bit of the world when he could, he had told the housekeeper, and to stay in a hotel for a change; and why not, as she said, when he could pay for his fancies?

When Oliver at length brought to an end a visit which had yielded much more than he expected, the housekeeper gladly undertook to mention his name (which happened to be Sam Beasley) to Mr. Potts, and to say that he would be calling about tea-time on the following day.

Oliver had now, he considered, abundant food for thought. More than ever was it necessary for him to set eyes on the mysterious Potts, and prove or disprove his identity with the man of the bungalow. A comparatively humble Potts who was the dead woman's brother was one thing; but a Potts with a private means, a Potts who was usually absent from home on Saturday nights — what of him?

Oliver turned these things over in a somewhat excited mind as he dealt slowly with a drink in the saloon bar of a hotel on the water-front. The place was fairly well patronised, and presently Oliver's eye lighted on a figure that he vaguely recognised. Not half an hour before, as he took leave of Potts's housekeeper on the doorstep, he had unconsciously noted a man who was strolling past at the time; a small, lean man, deeply sunburned, neat-moustached, with something in his bearing suggestive rather of the army than of seafaring. Now this small man, catching Oliver's eye, nodded pleasantly and brought his own drink to the table where the reporter sat.

"I saw you were making a call just now at Arthur Potts's place," the small man said without preamble. "Friend of yours, no doubt?"

Oliver regarded him gravely. "I don't know," he said, after a moment's silence, "that that's any

business of yours. It may be." For his lively mind
had already formed a shrewd guess at the small
man's business.

His guess was at once and rather surprisingly
confirmed. The small man handed him a card
bearing the name of Inspector C. F. S. Oates, and
in a lower corner the words, "Ministry of the In-
terior, Cairo."

Oliver gazed at the man blankly. "Cairo!" he
ejaculated.

"Capital of the Independent Kingdom of
Egypt," the small man explained with a faint grin.
"But never mind that just now. I don't believe
you are a friend of Potts; you look like a decent
fellow. And if you were just making a friendly
call, why were you talking Yorkshire – and doing
it well, if I may say so – to the old woman?"

"I was talking Yorkshire well," Oliver answered, "because I come from Yorkshire."

"So do I," Inspector Oates retorted. "Here's to
it!"

The two honoured the toast.

"I also talked the speech of God's own shire,"
Oliver continued, "because if I had talked the
language you and I are talking now, that old girl
would never have thawed out to me, nor ever believed that I was on intimate terms with Arthur
Potts. Such are the difficulties of democracy in
this land of ours. Inspector, have a look at this."
He presented to the small man his own professional card.

The other glanced at it swiftly. "Yes," he said.
"I rather thought it might be that. I know about
that Jumbles case, of course; though I do come
from Egypt. But I wonder why you should be tak-

ing an interest in Geraldine Potts's brother."

"Why," countered Oliver, "are you taking an interest in me?"

"I take an interest," the Inspector replied, "in a lot of people who take an interest in Arthur Potts. Well, I suppose I shall see you on the landing-stage tomorrow morning bright and early."

"I intend to meet Potts," Oliver said.

"Do you? I doubt if you will," Inspector Oates said coolly. "You'll see him, I dare say, if having a look at his fatal beauty is any good to you." And with that he finished his drink, nodded to the reporter, and went briskly out.

It was a well-filled passenger-steamer that came to rest at the landing-stage the next morning at half past six. Among the small crowd awaiting it, Oliver took up a position close to Inspector Oates, who favoured him with a brief nod. The gangways clattered into place, a squad of porters invaded the boat, and the passengers began their slow procession from the decks to the Customs shed. Almost at once Oliver caught sight of the scar-faced man of the bungalow, the veritable Potts, in steward's uniform, struggling with a heavy kit-bag and smaller chattels, and followed by a tall thin foreign-looking personage, evidently the owner of the baggage, whose opulence was vouched for by an astrakhan-lined overcoat. The Customs examination passed without event, and soon the steward was installing the tall man's effects in a first-class compartment of the waiting London train. The Inspector, Oliver noted, had never taken his eye off the pair for an instant since they first appeared, and was still watching them closely from a little distance among the hurrying crowd on the platform.

The tall man took his seat; a tip was gratefully received by Potts; and the tall man also handed to him, with an air that said, "Are these any good to you?" a few crumpled French newspapers and a bright-covered magazine. At that moment Inspector Oates raised his right hand above his head; and the next moment two burly men closed in on Potts. One of them spoke to him briefly, and the steward's yellow face turned grey. The Inspector, pressing forward, now took from the man's unresisting hand the papers just given to him, and slightly opened the crumpled pages. One glance was enough. He raised his hand again, and two more burly men stepped to the door of the compartment where the tall passenger sat. He also was briefly addressed; he descended to the platform, grim-faced and silent; and immediately the two culprits, held by either arm, were marched off to the harbour police-station with Inspector Oates jauntily bringing up the rear.

An hour later, sitting at his breakfast in the South-Western Hotel, Inspector Oates not only consented to receive Oliver, but invited him to join in the meal. The Inspector was in high good humour, and had no objection to talking, unofficially, of the morning's *coup*. "There's nobody here can haul me over the coals for it," he explained. "My chief in Cairo wants publicity for this job of ours."

He spoke of the ravages of the drug-traffic in Egypt, with its half-million addicts; of the Nar-

cotics Bureau set up by Russell Pasha, and of that
officer's policy of tracing the supplies to their
source and setting the police of other countries
on the track of the actual organisers of the trade,
the "men up above." The Inspector had been
sent to get in touch with Scotland Yard, where he
found that among those suspected as retail dis-
tributors was a steamboat steward, Potts. A clear
case had just been established against this man;
a statement had been obtained from one of his
clients. But his arrest had been postponed while
Inspector Oates, with his specialist knowledge of
the Continental gangs, went down to keep him
under observation in Southampton, in le Havre
and during the journeys between.

He had succeeded, unexpectedly, at the very
outset. Potts he had recognized that morning from
his description; but the tall foreigner was well
known to him as one Crescenzi, an Austrian, who
was known to be deep in the drug-traffic, but had
never been caught with the goods. The arrest of
Potts as soon as the papers changed hands involved no risk, for Potts was "for it" already; and
the moment the Inspector found among the newspapers and in the magazine the flat packages,
bookshaped and sealed, for which he was looking, Crescenzi was "for it," too. Also his big kit-
bag, with its false bottom, had well rewarded the
spirit of inquiry.

Oliver sighed with happiness. It was a beautiful story; and it was his alone. "There's just one
thing," he said. "I wanted Potts to have been in
the neighbourhood of Brighton on the evening of
Saturday, the seventh, the date of the Jumbles
crime."

"You can't pin it on him," Inspector Oates declared with decision. "Potts went on his dope-rounds twice a week in London, meeting his clients at places arranged by 'phone the same day.

"Either he would take the 7:30 back to Southampton, or if it was a Saturday, stay the night in town. On the evening you mention, Potts and a lady friend were enjoying the film 'Let's All Get Divorced,' at the Radiant Palace."

IX

BOND STREET OR BROAD STREET?

by anthony berkeley

Oliver had gone to Southampton. For once Beryl Blackwood sincerely missed him. There was no one else with whom she could talk over the subject which was now obsessing her mind, this matter of the Broad Street dagger and the mysterious "Deadman" who had been named as the purchaser of it.

Not, indeed, that any further discussion with Oliver seemed likely to prove profitable, Beryl thought as she sat over her solitary lunch. Oliver had disappointed her. At first, when she had told him of the incident yesterday, he had appeared just as struck by it, and indeed perturbed, as herself. Then gradually, almost as if he had been persuading himself, his view of its significance had gradually weakened and weakened: until in the end he had positively waved her fears and suspicions aside. It was impossible, he had assured her, that the incident could be anything more than a coincidence. It was ridiculous to suppose that Redman, of all people, was mixed up in the affair. She was letting her imagination run away with her.

At the time Oliver's conviction had influenced her. With his absence her fears had returned. It was *not* impossible that Redman should be mixed up in the affair, any more than it was impossible that cheerful young Johnson, of all people, should be stabbed to death in a telephone-box in Victoria Station. And Johnson had so been stabbed. Anything was possible after that.

Besides, there was that question of Bond Street and Broad Street. It was ridiculous to call it nothing but a coincidence that a jade pin should actually have been bought in Broad Street, when it was Broad Street itself that Johnson had seemed to her to say. If there was a coincidence at all, surely it was the Bond Street pin, not the Broad Street one. And yet Hemingway had understood Johnson to say Bond Street, and from Bond Street the pin had materialised. It was all most confusing. Beryl drummed with her knuckles on the table and let her portion of cabinet pudding get cold as her mind darted from this possibility to that, and from that impossibility back to this.

"There was a customer last month . . ." the woman in the Broad Street shop had said. Last *month*. But Fisher had bought his pin at Araby's only the day before Geraldine Potts was stabbed with it. Could it be the same pin? Could this pin have traced a devious course from Broad Street to the unknown Deadman, from Deadman to Araby, from Araby to Fisher, from Fisher to Geraldine? But, then, the descriptions were different. Undoubtedly there were two pins at issue, not one. Then what made her so sure that this second pin was connected with the murder? The similarity of Deadman and Redman, and the description of the purchaser that fitted Redman so appallingly well. Nothing else. There simply was nothing else – always excepting her feeling that Johnson had said Broad Street on the telephone. Oliver had insisted almost too strongly that there was nothing else.

Oliver had been wrong. Beryl sat back in her chair with a jerk, almost upsetting the cup of coffee with her elbow. How stupid they had been – how incredibly *stupid*! There had been a clue all the time within their own knowledge – right under their noses, and neither of them had seen it. This was important, terribly important. The information must be placed in authoritative hands at once. Even Oliver would agree to that now. How maddening that he was away, he would have done the placing so much more competently than herself; Oliver never lost his head. Well, no matter; she must do it instead. She felt, absurdly, as though there was not a second to lose; but, of course, it was no use rushing off like a whirlwind that instant; the news-editor would not be back from his own lunch for another half-hour at least. With what patience she could, Beryl set herself to face the interval before she could transfer this new burden from her own shoulders to the broader ones of Hemingway.

The point which had suddenly assumed such an overwhelming importance was a casual remark which Oliver had made to her a day or two ago, when they had been discussing the case just after the discovery of the weapon by the police. "A jade pin," Oliver had nodded, with his air, sometimes a little irritating to Beryl, of knowing everything just a few minutes before anyone else did. "Yes, I've heard of that pin already." And he had gone on to tell her that Gladys Sharp, the maidservant at the bungalow, had happened to mention this pin in connection with her late mistress's temper. Gladys Sharp had tried it in her hair on the Friday afternoon, and Geraldine had "gone on at her like a fishwife." In other words, Mrs. Tracey had been in possession of a jade pin before Fisher had even bought his – a pin which had since vanished, and of which there was, so far as Beryl knew, no official cognisance whatever. And a pin, moreover, of which the murderer must be afraid: for who else could have caused it to vanish but the murderer, and why else should he have done so but because he was afraid of its existence becoming known? It seemed to Beryl now that she might hold in her hands, with this piece of information, the solution of the whole mystery.

The half-hour passed at last, and she presented herself at Hemingway's room, almost trembling with excitement and responsibility.

Hemingway looked up with an air of surprise as she closed the door softly behind her and came close to his desk. "Yes, Miss Blackwood?" he asked, curtly. "Anything special?"

"Very, Mr. Hemingway. I want to tell you something." Succinctly, coolly, and almost as competently as Oliver himself, Beryl put the news-editor in possession of the facts, and her ideas about the two pins.

Hemingway's reception of them was certainly more gratifying than Oliver's had been. Before she had spoken half a dozen sentences Beryl could see from his face that he was taking just as grave a view of the situation as she herself. He waited in silence until she had finished and then said: "Sit down, please, Miss Blackwood. This is a very serious thing you're telling me. I want to understand it exactly. Leaving this matter of the two pins for the moment, you say Johnson spoke to you on the telephone. Was that a mistake of the switchboard operator's? Did she give him the wrong extension number?"

Beryl seated herself in the chair opposite the desk, which Hemingway had indicated with a brief nod. She had glossed over as much as possible her conversation with Johnson on the telephone. True, it was not her fault that he should have asked for her before asking for his newseditor; but she knew that it was a bad breach of discipline and Hemingway was a strict disciplinarian.

"No," she said now, rather nervously. "I think Mr. Johnson must have asked for the number."

"Why?" Hemingway demanded.

"I – don't know," Beryl replied, lamely.

Hemingway frowned at her. "This was before he spoke to me?"

"Yes," Beryl admitted uncomfortably.

"He asked for you before he asked for me," Hemingway continued to frown. "I don't understand it in the least. Why did he do that?"

Beryl said nothing. If Hemingway really couldn't understand, then he was a fool, she was thinking mutinously; and in any case it was most unfair to frown at her as if it were her fault. She couldn't help it that young reporters preferred to talk to her than to their news-editors.

"How long did this conversation last?" Hemingway asked next.

"Oh, not more than a few seconds," Beryl said hurriedly, and not very truthfully. "It was really only a couple of sentences. And it was so curious because I did feel afterwards that he'd said Broad –"

"Why didn't you report it earlier, Miss Blackwood?"

Hemingway cut into this attempt to shift the point under discussion. "Even if it was only a couple of sentences, as you now say, you should have reported it at once, to me or Mr. Lucas." Mr. Lucas was the editor, to whom Beryl would never have dreamed of going direct, however important her mission.

"But I didn't realise it was anything serious, Mr. Hemingway," she protested. "I mean, when you understood Mr. Johnson to say Bond Street, and a dagger was found from Bond Street, naturally I thought I'd been mistaken . . ." Her voice trailed off. Beryl was on the carpet, and she did not like it. She had been anticipating praise for her astuteness and she was being blamed for stupidity. Mr. Hemingway was quite annoyed with her. It was most unfair.

"Anything is important in a case of murder," Hemingway told her sourly. "I should have thought your training here would have taught you that, at least. It was most remiss and foolish of you not to report this conversation the first minute after you heard of Johnson's death. Report it,

I mean, to somebody competent to deal with it — because I've no doubt," Hemingway sneered, "that as it's about the most confidential thing that will ever come your way, involving as it does now an important member of the staff, you've prattled about it to every Tom, Jane and Harriet about the place. In fact, it'll probably turn out that the only people in the building who haven't heard of it are Mr. Lucas and myself. It's a wonder to me that it hasn't got into the *Courier* by now." The *Courier* was the *Morning Star*'s own particular rival.

"I haven't!" Beryl retorted indignantly. "I don't 'prattle about the place,' Mr. Hemingway."

"Well, how many people have you told?" Hemingway asked, unmoved. "Eh?" he shot at her as she did not answer at once. "How many?"

"None!" Beryl squeaked hastily, in high alarm. Hemingway would never forgive her if she confessed to having told Oliver before himself; that would be a breach of discipline almost worse than Johnson's. Better sacrifice the truth than her post, and warn Oliver not to give her away. "I haven't told anyone."

"Then you've got more sense than I should have given you credit for," Hemingway conceded grudgingly. "And don't."

"Certainly not," Beryl said, clutching for her dignity. He was tapping idly on his desk with a paper-knife and frowning in a concentration of thought.

"I shall have to see this woman myself," he announced at last.

"Yes, do," Beryl agreed at once. "You'll know how to get ever so much more out of her than I

did. We all know," she added with timid propi-
tiation, "what a star crime reporter you used to
be, Mr. Hemingway."

"Uh-huh," muttered Hemingway absently.

Beryl sat in respectful silence, waiting for the
next remark.

It came in the form of a question, and a flood
of others after it. Hemingway proceeded to put
her through a searching examination of her story,
taking each section of it in turn and probing into
her mind and memory until she felt that she had
never had a thought which remained secret from
him.

"Yes," he said at last, "the more you tell me,
Miss Blackwood, the more convinced I become
that Johnson must have said 'Broad Street' to you.
At least, I can't conceive how you could have got
the name into your mind if he didn't. Broad —
Bond: they're not so much alike as to be mistaken
for each other."

"But you thought he said 'Bond,'" Beryl
pointed out.

"I thought so, certainly. But I may have taken
it for granted," Hemingway admitted — rather
handsomely, Beryl thought. "And this information of yours makes me doubtful. Anyhow, one of
us was obviously mistaken, and I certainly won't
say it wasn't I. Of course, you realise that the
whole case is altered now, from top to bottom? I
mean, even leaving Mr. Redman out of it for the
moment, the possibility of there being two pins
means that everything on which the police and
all of us have been working may turn out to be a
completely false basis, with the result that the

case will have to be reconstructed from A to Z?"

"Yes," Beryl said soberly. "I realise that only too well."

"Then I don't think I need impress on you the absolute necessity for secrecy," Hemingway said, more kindly. "You've done your part, now it's out of your hands. I shall consult with Mr. Lucas of course, and he may send for you to verify one or two points; but apart from that your best policy now is to forget that you ever knew anything."

"Yes," Beryl nodded. "You may not believe it, Mr. Hemingway, but I can keep a secret."

Hemingway smiled faintly. "As to Mr. Redman, it seems to me, as it did to you, the wildest surmise that he could possible be mixed up in it. Quite fantastic. After all, what is there but a coincidental similarity of name and appearance – a similarity that might apply to hundreds of people? But, of course, that doesn't mean that we mustn't look into it and the fact that we all like Mr. Redman and that he is a member of the staff here mustn't affect the matter."

"Of course not," Beryl agreed at once. This had been her own view. Oliver's expressed reluctance, and indeed refusal, to carry on any investigations that seemed to lead to a fellow-member of the staff had struck her as a narrow and misplaced loyalty.

"As I said," Hemingway was continuing, "I shall consult with Mr. Lucas as to the course we shall adopt, but he will almost certainly agree with my own idea, which is to have a few words with Mr. Redman myself. I can sound him in such a way that he won't have the least inkling that we suspect anything. But I must say," Hemingway added, in a more human tone, "it's a rotten job,

Miss Blackwood. I wish we could hush the whole thing up, but I suppose . . ." His intonation of the last words made them almost a question.

"It's horrible," Beryl agreed vehemently. "But it can't be hushed up, of course. After all, one has only to think of poor Mr. Johnson, and – and –" Her voice broke.

"Yes," said Hemingway soberly. "Yes."

There was a little silence.

The interview was obviously at an end. With considerable relief Beryl stood up and made her exit. In spite of the censure she had received, she felt at ease for the first time since leaving the Broad Street shop. Undoubtedly Oliver had for once not come up to scratch.

Left alone Hemingway continued for a few minutes to maintain an attitude of hard thought. Beryl's news, much though he would have deplored her failure to impart it, had placed him in an exceedingly awkward position. He was not quite sure how best to deal with it. Finally he shrugged his shoulders, as if at such ridiculous scruples, and rose to his feet with a slight sigh.

His eye fell on the huge desk which he and Redman shared. On either side, from floor to top, was a stack of drawers, not narrow as in the ordinary pedestal-desk, but wide and deep. The majority of them were devoted to the tools of their profession, reams of paper, indiarubbers, blue pencils and so on; but the bottom drawer on either side was reserved for their own private oddments, his on the right, Redman's on the left. Hemingway walked slowly over to the desk, opened the left-hand bottom drawer, and stood staring down into it.

At first sight it seemed to contain nothing but

the usual masculine litter – a couple of pipes, a pair of gloves, some letters, two or three snap-shots, a tobacco-tin, a box of cigarettes, and so on, filling it for at least half its depth. Hemingway leant down and slowly pushed the litter to the back of the drawer, exposing something that was underneath it. It was not apparently a very im-portant object which he thus brought to light, nothing more than a sheet of greyish cardboard which had been cut to fit the edges of the drawer and serve as a lining. He inserted his thumbnail under the front edge, lifted it, and drew out the sheet.

It was obvious that the sheet could not have covered the whole of the bottom of the drawer. It was not deep enough, by eight or ten inches. Hemingway examined the back edge. It, too, had been cut by a knife; but whereas the sides and front were smooth, the back edge was rough and in places jagged, as if it had been ripped in haste.

Hemingway stood for a moment staring at the cardboard in his hand, and most particularly at the back edge. Then he walked swiftly over to the door, locked it, carried the cardboard over to the fireplace, and began swiftly to slice it into slivers with his pen-knife into the grate. Leaning down, he put a match to the little pile and bent over it, poking it with a pencil, until it had burnt into ash.

The police had made a special note of the fact that the "Out of Order" notice, which had been hung on the door of the telephone-box at Victoria Station, had been made of cardboard of a partic-ular greyish tint.

X

BERYL TAKES THE CONSEQUENCES

by clemence dane

Beryl Blackwood heaved a sigh of profound satisfaction. Once again it was Saturday night and once again she had her flat to herself. Her satisfaction was no reflection on the nice girl with whom she shared her small home. Nevertheless, the nicest thing about the nice girl was the fact that the nice girl went home for weekends, because then Beryl and the puppy could do exactly as they liked. While he ratted in the coal-bin she cooked far more food than was at all necessary on the not too remote chance that someone might drop in; to put it plainly, that Oliver might drop in. She had not seen him for a week. And when he had 'phoned her he had been terse and breathless, which meant that he had more worries on his mind, and sooner or later would want to tell her about it. She did hope he would come; for she, too, had a worry to discuss with him.

113

The more she thought over the interview with Hemingway the less pleased was she at the part which she had played. There was no use in deceiving herself. She might as well face it. She, a modern woman with a vote, a flat, a latch-key, views on life and literature, and an independent soul, had let herself be bullied. And not even by a man whom she liked! She had been in the right: she had behaved with absolute correctness, yet that sour prig, that austere devil of correctness, Hemingway, had actually flustered her into a silly lie. Wasn't it monstrous?

The more she thought of that feeble lie the more annoyed, angry, furious she felt — annoyed with herself, angry with Hemingway, and really furious with Denis Oliver whose preoccupation with his own theories, whose refusal to consider her discovery important had led her to Hemingway. She saw now how unwise she had been. She should never have gone to Hemingway. But having gone she should not have let herself be intimidated by Hemingway. Above all she should not have lied. What possessed her to say that she had told no one of her Broad Street adventure when she knew perfectly well that she had told Denis? She was ashamed of herself. She didn't do that sort of thing. She didn't know what in the world Denis would say to her when she told him, for, of course, though she didn't want to tell him, she would have to tell him all about it, Hemingway or no Hemingway. They were practically engaged. You couldn't have secrets from a next-door-to-husband. She wished he would come.

As time went by she found herself listening to the occasional steps of passers-by in the street below with an intensity that surprised herself, and when the telephone bell rang she rushed to it very joyfully. It meant, she supposed, that he couldn't come — but how nice of him to ring up!

"Hullo, Denis, my dear, is that you?" said she rashly. And then, to the excited little animal beside her: "Down, puppy. Be quiet, can't you?" But the puppy wouldn't be quiet and she had to apologise to the crackling telephone: "Here, hold on a minute. I must just shut up the dog." Then, in one impetuous sweep she had set down the receiver, swept up the puppy, tossed it into her bedroom, shut the door and returned, breathless, with: "Hullo! Hullo! Denis, are you there?" And then knew that she had been a fool again. It wasn't Denis: and she had given herself and her private affairs away to no less a person than her own chief. She hurriedly did her best.

"Oh how stupid of me. It's Mr. Hemingway, isn't it?"

There was no direct answer, only a pause, the crackle of the telephone, then the voice at the other end, "Hullo-ing" again as if it had not heard her.

"Hullo! Hullo! Is that you, Miss Blackwood? Redman speaking."

"Oh!" Her surprise made her forget her annoyance. "Oh, is it Mr. Redman? Funny! For a moment I thought it was Mr. Hemingway."

At that there was a laugh, reassuring, friendly. "Did you? I'm sorry to disturb you. I hope you haven't visitors?" said the telephone.

"Oh no, that's all right," said Beryl quickly. "I'm alone" — then, with an uncertainty that surprised herself: "It *is* Mr. Redman, isn't it?"

"Of course. Why?"

"Your voice doesn't sound like yourself, some-how."

"Only a cold," said the voice.

"Oh yes. I forgot." Silly of her – as if she hadn't sympathised with him only that morning. He had some inhalant of hers in his desk at that moment. But she still had the oddest feeling that the in-flections of the voice were not natural, but well – a cold does alter a voice, of course.

All this flashed through her mind as she lis-tened to Redman, a rather less business-like Red-man than usual. That, she supposed, was because he was conscious of breaking into her precious free time with his "Hullo's".

"Hullo! Hullo! Are you there still, Miss Black-wood? It's a shame to worry you at this time of night, but I've just seen Hemingway. I under-stand you've got information for us."

"What?" said she sharply, for she was startled. The need for secrecy had been so drummed into her at the recent interview, that she could hardly credit the fact that Hemingway had talked.

"How do you know?" she said uncertainly. "Did Mr. Hemingway say so?"

"Yes. I understand that you had a talk with Johnson that you've only just reported."

"But Mr. Hemingway told me not to mention it to anyone," said she.

"I daresay, but he naturally discussed it with me," said the voice, huffily, and was again ov-ertaken by a fit of coughing, before it resumed more hoarsely than ever: "Now look here, Miss Blackwood, I know you must be sick of the sub-ject, but would you mind going over the conversation with me once again? The conversation, I mean, that you had with Johnson."

"But I told Mr. Hemingway all I knew," she protested.

"I know, but it occurred to me that in the circumstances —" his laugh rang pleasantly.

"What circumstances?" returned Beryl uncomfortably.

"Oh, my dear Miss Blackwood, it was pretty obvious that poor Johnson talked to you at some length."

"Well, I'll tell you anything I can," she said doubtfully. "But, honestly. I think I've told everything."

"I'm sure you think you did."

"I know I did."

"Miss Blackwood, in your not-too-remote nursery did you never play Hunt-the-Thimble?"

"What d'you mean?"

"My dear Miss Blackwood, when you've satisfied yourself that the thimble isn't in a certain corner then, if you are wise, you search that corner again. Now look here —"

"Yes?"

"I've been interviewing the operator. Is it a fact that Johnson had a three-minute talk with you before you passed him on to Hemingway?"

Beryl, more chagrined than ever, was not yet able to keep a certain unwilling admiration out of her voice. "You're more thorough than Mr. Hemingway," she said.

"He did then? Don't think I'm blaming you. Perfectly natural. But it occurred to me that, though you told Mr. Hemingway the gist of the conversation, you probably did not report the exact phrases that Johnson used. Could you try and remember exactly what he said? The actual words, however unimportant they seem to you, might help."

"He didn't say much," said she unwillingly.

"Never mind. Try and remember everything."

She hesitated.

The voice showed impatience.

"Well?" it said.

"Well, I couldn't hear him very plainly," she began. "He said he was speaking from the farmhouse and that he'd got a real scoop. And that he'd found the weapon and thought he could identify it. But you know all this from Mr. Hemingway."

"Never mind. I want your version. How did he propose to identify it? I mean the Chinese pin?"

"He thought he'd seen one like it in a shop," said Beryl.

"How did he describe the shop?"

Again the voice thickened, and again it flashed over her mind, "how odd he sounds tonight," but she answered: "Well, the line was bad. But he said a junk shop in Broad Street."

"You're not sure?"

"Pretty sure."

"Why are you so sure?" asked the voice.

"Well, he spelt it."

There was a silence. "Hullo?" said Beryl into the receiver at last. And got no answer. The telephone had gone dead.

"He'll come through again, if he wants to," she thought philosophically. "It's up to him. I'm not going to bother." And she went back again to the kitchen, letting out the dog as she passed the bedroom door and saying to herself: "Ten o'clock.

Won't come now. He might, though. Perhaps I'd better lay supper in case." So she set out her cold fare and chopped her herbs and broke her eggs into a salted, peppered, mustard-dabbed basin so that the omelette could be whisked together the moment he came, glancing over and again at the clock as she did so. Funny that Redman hadn't rung up again. Funny that something always went wrong with the line when you really wanted to use it. Five-and-twenty-to-eleven. No, Denis wouldn't come now. She might as well go to bed.

Disappointed, yet vexed with herself for being disappointed, she was beginning slowly to put away the untouched supper-dishes when, very quietly, a bell rang. Not the telephone bell, as she first thought, for she always confused the two. No, it was the welcome ringing of the flat-door bell.

Gaily the puppy ran ahead of her down the passage into the murky little hall; but as she stooped to fumble with the bolt it began to growl, and as she threw back the door with an impetuous word of welcome it ran, still snarling, out on to the dark landing. Then her words stopped abruptly. There was nobody there.

She came out, peered down the staircase, calling: "Who's there? Is that you, Denis?"

As if in answer, there was a rustle on the turn of the stair above her, and a yelp from the dog. Then, as she turned, a darkness rushed upon her: she put out a hand to ward off that cloud of darkness, was aware of a smother of cloth upon her face, a blow and a sizzle of light inside her head, and then she ceased to be aware of anything at all.

But the puppy was aware that something had
gone wrong, badly wrong with the universe. The
puppy, until it reached the haven of Beryl's flat,
regular meals, irregular exercise and far too many
chocolates, had had a hard life. For it had been
stolen long before it reached the animal shop, and
knew all about hob-nailed boots and rows in the
darkness. The one furious kick recalled old times,
and it raced yelping down the stairs to crouch in
the dark hall till its fright had worn off. But time
went by and there was no familiar, soft voice to
call it up the stairs again, but instead there came
presently a heavy, hurried footfall that the puppy
recognised. "Not a second kick, thank you,"
thought the puppy. Yelping terror, it fled once
more into a night sparsely inhabited by passing
trouser-legs, the rush of taxis, damp, fog, cold, and
would have continued indefinitely splaying forward through the darkness if it had not met in
mid-passage the bliss of a familiar smell. The
dithered puppy pulled up short and greeted with
jumpings and pawings, and a flurry of tail and
high barks of relief, the one creature in the world
that the puppy preferred before its mistress, the
man with buttery boots, the safe man who said
"Basket!" and was obeyed.

Oliver hurrying along, snapped his finger at
the puppy with a smile, that turned in an instant
to recognition and the quick disquiet of a lover.
What was Beryl's beast doing at this distance from
Beryl's flat? Was she out? Was that why he had
had no answer when he rang her up ten minutes
ago? Really, if Beryl was out when she had prom-
ised to be in, it would be extraordinarily incon-
siderate.   .

He hurried on, to be reassured by light streaming as usual from the sitting-room window on the upper floor. So Beryl was in then. He hurried up the stairs, while the puppy, with unusual caution, slunk at his heels. But, though the light was on and he rang loudly, Beryl did not come rushing. He rang: he knocked: he knocked: he rang. At last he snapped on his lighter, but he searched in vain for the expected note: "Back in five minutes." Finally, he stooped to the letter-box and proceeded to call through it:

"Beryl! I say, Beryl, I say, where are you? Nothing wrong, is there? Beryl!"

No answer. The puppy whined, and Oliver, more worried than he cared to acknowledge, knelt again to see if he could catch a glimpse of the flat itself through the letter-box. His foot slipped: he steadied himself with one hand on the floor and brought it away, sticky. A moment he hesitated, then, with a glance of impatience at the broken light — he had told Beryl only last week that she should ask the caretaker for a new bulb — he snapped on his lighter and once more shone it upon his hand. Then, horrified, he stooped to examine the floor, for he had stepped in blood: and his hand was red with it.

He stood a moment experiencing the sickness that a woman feels at the sight of a child on the edge of a cliff. Then, for his sense told him that no assault upon the strong little door would avail, dashed down the staircase, still attended by the obsequious puppy, and out into the road where his subconscious mind had noted a night-watchman's shanty ten yards away with its lamps, its glowing brazier, its encircling ropes and stack of tools.

He secured a crowbar, shouting as he did so

incoherent directions concerning help and police to the startled watchman, dashed back across the road, tore up the stairs, and with a few blows had the door open, and was racing down the passage.

It was a shock to find the brightly lighted sitting-room empty, and yet a relief, till he thought of the bedroom. The bedroom was in darkness, and he fumbled with shaking hands for the switch, calling once more, "Beryl, what's up?" as the room leaped into being. But once more he stared at a tidy emptiness. Only the kitchen was left: and sure enough the kitchen was not empty, though it was quiet. The smell of gas filled it, and in front of the practical little oven, Beryl lay huddled, her chin on the oven grid, her body collapsed, her hands trailing, and her cheek smeared with brown grease.

And then, before he could do more than pull her clear of the death-trap, steps and voices sounded loudly in the passage, and the night watchman and a policeman entered together.

XI

INSPECTOR SMART'S NASTY JAR

by freeman wills crofts

Reporter Oliver grew cold with dread when he found Beryl Blackwood lying unconscious with her head in the gas oven in her flat. But he did not hesitate for a moment. Laying the helpless girl on the floor, he vigorously applied artificial respiration, while he yelled to the policeman to ring up, first a doctor, and then Scotland Yard.

Within half an hour Inspector Smart was at the flat. Beryl had just regained consciousness, and she was able to gasp out her story. Smart at once saw that here was a very deliberate attempt at murder. That it had not so eventuated was due to one of those extraordinary oversights which criminals seem unable to avoid. The assailant had forgotten to put a coin in the meter, and the gas had been cut off in the nick of time!

Smart next made two calls; to the Yard for fingerprint experts to examine objects which the would-be murderer might have touched, and to the local exchange to trace the call Beryl had received earlier in the evening. Then he hurried to the *Morning Star* office.

A good deal of progress had been made with the case since the conference over which Chief Inspector Bradford had presided, when Tracey, Fisher, Potts, Redman and Oliver had still remained suspects. Three of these had now been eliminated. On the night of the Victoria crime Fisher had been able to prove that he really had done a good three hours' work between nine o'clock and midnight, while Oliver had been seen at Oxford Circus at ten o'clock. On the night of the Jumbles murder Potts was in London. It was believed that innocence of one crime implied innocence of the other and this, therefore, reduced the suspects to Tracey and Redman. Further, it was now believed that Tracey, as such, had no independent existence, but that someone else had masqueraded under that name. The chief's suggestion that Tracey might actually be Redman still remained a possibility, those who had seen Tracey being uncertain whether Redman was or was not he. It was true that the police had been unable to bring the purchase of the Broad Street pin home to Redman. The old lady of the junk shop had failed to identify him as her customer. Smart, however, remained impressed by Beryl's discoveries, and when he heard Redman's name mentioned in connection with the attack on Beryl, he hugged himself, thinking he saw the end of his case.

When Smart reached the *Morning Star* office it was to find his hopes dashed. There was overwhelming proof that Redman had been in the building during the whole evening. This discovery left Smart gasping. Redman was innocent of the attack on Beryl. Who then was guilty?

Then Smart remembered that Beryl had said that the unknown sounded like Hemingway. Could she possibly have been right? Smart grew aghast as he saw where this was going to lead. If Hemingway had bought the pin and planned the attack on Beryl to prevent this becoming known — why then, it followed that Hemingway must be their man; that he must be guilty of the murders; that he must really be Tracey!

Then Smart saw something which gave him to think even more furiously. On that very day Hemingway had received a piece of information which, had he been guilty, would have scared him into fits. He had learned that Johnson had told Beryl about the Broad Street pin. If, now, Hemingway had really bought a pin in Broad Street, he must have realised that this information of Beryl's would hang him if it became known. He would be taken to the shop, where someone would identify him as the purchaser. He would be taken to the Jumbles, where someone would identify him as Tracey. Hence the need for silencing Beryl. Then Smart saw that all this speculation was valueless. There was the man's alibi. Hemingway was at least not guilty of the Victoria murder, because he wasn't there at the time.

Smart got back to Beryl's flat to find Chief Inspector Bradford had just arrived.

"What have you done, Smart?" the chief asked.

Smart explained, tentatively mentioning his speculations. To his amazement the chief was enthusiastic.

"You have got it!" Bradford cried. "Hemingway's our man all right."

"But his alibi, sir. It is impossible."

"Look here, Smart," the chief said slowly, "it was Hemingway, because if Redman's out of it, there is no one else it could have been. Is Hemingway innocent of the attack on Beryl?"

"I have not found out yet, sir."

"Then find out, and look here again. If Hemingway cannot clear himself of the attack on Beryl, you take it from me he is guilty of the murders as well. As for the alibi," the chief shrugged, "he has diddled you over it. Try it again."

Smart knew otherwise. He was very certain he had not been diddled over the alibi. Curse the chief's nonsense! However, he took a taxi to Hemingway's house in Hampstead.

"Evening, Inspector. What is the matter now?" Hemingway greeted him.

"Still the same, sir," Smart returned pleasantly. "The chief sent me over to see you. He thought you might be interested to know that the attack on Beryl Blackwood was a failure. She's recovering."

It was a bow drawn at a venture. Smart smiled easily, but his keen eyes never left the other's face. And there they read the riddle. Hemingway blenched as if he had been struck, while the blood slowly drained from his face. Then he pulled himself together.

"The attack on Beryl Blackwood?" he repeated in somewhat shaky tones. "Good heavens, Inspector! This is news to me. What attack?"

Smart was full of apologies. "You have not heard, sir? We thought you would have been advised at once from the office." He went on to give details, ending up: "Fortunately there's a clue. Miss Blackwood was known to have refused one of her many suitors this evening, and he was seen in the neighbourhood about the time of the crime."

Hemingway clearly was puzzled. Smart, however, was so obviously suspicious of this rejected suitor that relief began to show on his face. By the time Smart took his leave, Hemingway's manner was almost normal.

From the nearest call office Smart reported to the chief.

"Right, we'll watch him," Bradford returned. "Keep an eye on the house till I send someone to relieve you. Then go into that alibi."

With a bad grace Smart prepared to obey. Nonsense, that about questioning the alibi. In his mind he went once again over the steps he had taken to test it, only to become more than ever convinced that it was sound.

He had begun by reconstructing the crime. With a fast car and accompanied by a sergeant he had gone to Victoria, reaching the telephone box at 10:04, the hour of the crime. The sergeant had thrown himself on the floor of the box, and Smart had hurriedly pushed the body clear of the door, run through the pockets, hung up a cardboard notice, and shut the door. Moving just not quickly enough to attract attention, he had reached the car, and at once they had set off. At Hampstead they had parked in a side street, as Smart did not believe Hemingway would have left his car outside his house, and they hurried on foot to the door. That had brought it to 10:23. Two minutes more for Hemingway to open the door, take off his things and reach the sitting-room would have made it 10:25. Under no conceivable circumstances, therefore, could the man have got back by 10:10.

Smart had then checked the time at which Hemingway had reached home. He had arrived from the office just slightly late for dinner at 8:15. He had called to the others to go on, which they had done, and he had joined them shortly. After dinner he had gone out. He had returned about 10:10 and had at once turned on his set. He was an enthusiastic amateur radio expert. Some symphony music was coming through, but not clearly, and Hemingway had gone to get some tools to go over his connections. Just after he had left the room the 10:15 time signal had come through. Hemingway had come back and begun to work, but unfortunately had knocked down and broken one of his valves, putting the set out of commission.

This was vouched for by Mrs. Hemingway, the governess, and Mrs. Hemingway's mother, who was on a visit. The incident was remembered because of the old lady's disappointment at not hearing the remainder of the music.

Smart was satisfied that the ladies were telling the truth, not only from their manner, but because he was convinced that they did not know what lay behind the questions. All the same, before accepting the alibi, he obtained a number of corroborative facts. First, the sitting-room clock was with the time signal. Second, the sitting-room and hall clocks struck together, not only on that evening, but on the evenings before and after. Third, the clocks were correct, because Mrs. Hemingway, who had been down town on both that day and the day following, had checked them on each occasion with the town clocks by means of her wrist watch. Fourth, there was no doubt about the evening, as it was that of the Lord Mayor's Show, and fifth, on that evening the Regional programme had been symphony music, up to 10:15.

And now, in spite of all these cumulative proofs, Smart was asked to believe he had been diddled over the alibi. Well, he just hadn't, and that was all there was to it.

For some hours Smart was like a bear with a particularly sore head. What could he do that he had not already done? Every possibility of fake seemed to have been ruled out by his previous investigation. He didn't see that he had left a single loophole for error.

Then it occurred to him that there was one check which he had not completed. He had asked Mrs. Hemingway and the governess what the music was which had come through on the evening in question, but they had not been able to tell him. Thinking the point immaterial, he had left it at that. Now he thought he would put the same question to old Mrs. Kent, Mrs. Hemingway's mother. She had been disappointed that the music had been cut off, so presumably she knew what it was. Inside the hour Smart was at her house in Surbiton, to which she had returned.

Mrs. Kent was able to answer the question. The music was Beethoven's Fifth Symphony. And not only that, but she was able to tell him the exact part which was played during the five or more minutes between the turning on of the set and the breaking of the valve. She remembered distinctly hearing the long-sustained note between the third and fourth movements. It had come through just before the set broke down.

Smart's next call was at Savoy Hill. At the B.B.C. headquarters he saw a polite member of the Music Department.

"I want to know," he said, "at what hour Beethoven's Fifth Symphony was broadcast on the night of November 9?"

The polite young man looked up papers. "I'm afraid it wasn't on our programmes that night at all," he answered.

Smart's heart sank suddenly. "Was it broadcast from any other station that night?" he asked.

Further searchings of papers; then: "What about this? Radio-Paris; a Beethoven night. Last item, the Fifth Symphony. There you are, Inspector."

A cold misgiving was creeping down Smart's spine, but he went on: "Can you tell me at what hour that broadcast began?"

"Can't tell that here, but I'll ring up Paris if you'll stand the damage."

"Go ahead."

Within an hour Smart had his information. The symphony had begun at 10:10.

The cold misgiving was growing into an icy certainty. With set teeth Smart went ahead. After a good deal of trouble he got one of the B.B.C. conductors to play through the symphony from the beginning as far as the sustained note. He found it took just twenty minutes.

From all this it followed that the sustained note had been played in Paris on the evening of the crime at almost exactly 10:30. If Mrs. Kent were right, the Paris programme, and not the Regional, had been heard in Hemingway's drawing-room — and at 10:30, not 10:15.

Smart swore bitterly. If Hemingway returned to his house five minutes before that piece of music was heard, it meant that he had arrived at 10:25. If so, the alibi was a fake, and he could have murdered Johnson at Victoria!

But there were still the clocks and that cursed time signal to be explained. Smart returned to Hemingway's house and started a fresh enquiry. First he concentrated on the clocks, and rigorous questioning resulted in two discoveries. The first was that on the evening of the Victoria crime the kitchen clock had mysteriously stopped during dinner. The second was that at bedtime the governess found her wrist watch stopped, with the mainspring broken. Neither she nor Mrs. Hemingway wore their wrist watches with evening dress, and they had dressed regularly during Mrs. Kent's visit. Their watches were therefore in their bedrooms between dinner and bedtime.

Smart sat down in Hemingway's study and wrestled with the problem. For a long time he could get no light then suddenly he realised the significance of the fact that Hemingway had come in late for dinner and had called to his wife to go on without him.

Smart saw it at last. At the beginning of dinner the entire household would be assembled in the dining room. What could be easier than for Hemingway then to put all the clocks back a quarter of an hour?

Except the kitchen clock. If the servant had got

dinner for 8:15 and then gone out and seen that it was only 8:05, the fat would be in the fire.

But what about the governess's watch? Smart saw that if Hemingway put back the clocks he must put them on again. And when? Only in the middle of the night. But in the middle of the night Hemingway could not get at the governess's watch. Hence the watch must be stopped.

Still there remained that exasperating business of the time-signal.

The ladies had said that Hemingway had just left the drawing-room when the signal came through. Hemingway must therefore have been in the hall at that moment. Smart therefore concentrated on the hall. And then he saw it.

Hanging on a hat-stand was one of those children's toy whips which have a whistle at the end of the handle. Smart blew it and there was a very realistic representation of a B.B.C. signal! Six blasts outside the open door of the drawing-room would have done the trick.

And now Smart saw why Hemingway had smashed his valve. He had to hide the fact that no news followed the time-signal.

Here, Smart saw, was the truth at last. His face was grim as he thought of the coming interview with his chief.

But all Bradford said when Smart had finished was: "Well, that's what happened. But you've not proved it. Go and get up a case that you can take into court."

Smart, bitterly humbled, went out to do so.

XII

THE FINAL SCOOP

by dorothy l. sayers

In the gateway of New Scotland Yard, Inspector Smart encountered Oliver.

"Hullo!" said the latter. "The very man I was coming to see. I have got news for you. About Hemingway. I have discovered that Hemingway was Tracey."

The Inspector took Oliver's arm in an affectionate grip. "Come inside," said he.

"I am on the staff of the *Daily Courier* now, you know," observed Oliver, as the two men entered Smart's office. "I had to chuck the *Morning Star* when I thought that things were pointing to Redman. Couldn't very well stay there and work up a story against one of the chiefs, you know. It is a bit awkward, anyhow," went on Oliver, "but after that damned cowardly business the other night, I don't care *who* suffers. It made a very good story, though," he added, with wistful pride.

"Yes, I read it," said the Inspector. "I hope Miss Blackwood is recovering all right."

"Doing well," returned Oliver; "in fact, we are thinking of getting married in the New Year."

The Inspector congratulated him. "But about Hemingway," he hinted.

"Oh, yes," said Oliver. "Well, when we found out that it couldn't have been Redman who attacked Miss Blackwood, I began to wonder if it really was Hemingway after all. And that led me to wonder if Hemingway could possibly be the mysterious weekender who worked east of Charing Cross. After all, he had no alibi for the night of the Jumbles murder."

"No," said Smart. "He said he had gone to the pictures and come home at about eleven o'clock. We could not prove that one way or another. But if he was Tracey, we have got to account for the other weekends he spent at the bungalow. We checked that up and found that when he was not at home he was playing golf with a man called Pyecraft near Guildford. Pyecraft corroborated that all right. He used to fetch Hemingway in his car. Mrs. Hemingway knew all about it."

"Very likely," said Oliver. "But you didn't take Pyecraft into your confidence. I did. The obliging Pyecraft has been covering up Hemingway's peccadilloes for some time. His job was to fetch Hemingway on Saturday mornings, take him home, give him lunch and a round of golf, and then speed him by train to an unknown destination, no question asked. If enquiring wives rang up Mr. Hemingway was staying with Mr. Pyecraft; he was out at the moment but would ring up as soon as he came in. Hemingway never failed to ring up either — regularly every evening. Said he was speaking from Pyecraft's house. So kind and attentive of him, wasn't it?"

"Humph!" said Smart, rather mortified.

"I don't think Pyecraft is an accessory," pursued Oliver, "only a bit of an ass. He said he never knew where Hemingway went on Saturdays — only that he kept a little love-nest somewhere. Apparently Hemingway told him once that he had picked the girl up in Hyde Park. Pyecraft thought he really was desperately fond of the young woman."

"I see," said Smart. "Well, that certainly clears up one difficulty. Now, if Hemingway really was Tracey, what exactly do you think happened down there at the Bungalow? Those two pins, for instance — what about them?"

"This is how I have doped it out," replied Oliver. "Hemingway picked up Geraldine Potts, as Pyecraft says, and Geraldine fancied she had got on to a good thing. No doubt she thought that a house of her own near Brighton, with a regular allowance and a girl to do the work, sounded a darned sight better than the hat shop. But the Jumbles is not Brighton — not by a long chalk, and we have got the servant-girl's word for it that Geraldine soon got fed up. Of course, Hemingway could only be there off and on at weekends, so while the cat was away, the little mouse started to play — with our friend Fisher.

"Well, now, the pins. Hemingway bought the first pin in Broad Street —"

"Stop a minute," interrupted Smart. "Why did he call himself Dedham or Deadman when he bought it?"

"Sheer habit of caution, I think," said Oliver. "The woman suddenly asked for a name, and he gave the first that came uppermost. I expect he really did say Redman. He may even have had a dim idea of using the slight likeness between himself and Redman as a kind of cover for his activities in case anybody suspected a link between the Jumbles Bungalow and the *Morning Star*. I do know that when he went down to the Jumbles he used to brush his moustache down over his mouth as Redman does, instead of waxing it up in his usual style. Pyecraft laughed about it – said you wouldn't believe the difference it made to him. The horn rims were part of the Redman outfit, too – he always used to wear pincenez at one time."

"I see," said Smart. "Well, all right. He buys the pin in Broad Street and gives it to Geraldine. Well now, since we got your story about the Broad Street pin, we have been putting Fisher through it. He says he saw the pin one day at the bungalow and asked Geraldine about it. Geraldine did not seem to think much of it, until he told her that it was valuable and that there ought to be a pair to it. Then she becomes crazy to get hold of the second pin – and Fisher says he will see what he can do. Right! Well, off he goes, and on Friday, November 6, he finds the second pin at Araby's in Bond Street and posts it down to Geraldine. *And* he puts in a letter to say, how about him coming along next evening to claim a bit of reward and all that? You get me. Hemingway – Tracey that is – was not supposed to be coming down that Saturday, so he thinks that will be quite okay."

"Why wasn't Hemingway coming down?" asked Oliver.

"In my opinion," said Smart, "he was beginning to have his suspicions of Miss Geraldine and her friend Fisher, and thought he'd like to pop down unexpected-like and see what she was up to."

"That's quite likely," said Oliver. "Then he'd get there — say at seven-thirty or eight, and he'd find her all dolled-up with her pair of hair pins, waiting for kind, rich Mr. Fisher."

"That's it," Smart nodded. "And he'd see she was nervous and none too pleased to see him, and he'd ask what was the matter with her, and then he'd notice the second pin and ask who gave her that. She'd tell him that kind, rich Mr. Fisher bought it for her in Bond Street. And then there'd be a regular bust-up."

"That's right," agreed Oliver. "And he'd snatch Fisher's pin out of her hair and stab her with it."

"No, no," said Smart. "The pin Johnson found was the Broad Street pin — he recognised it."

"So he did. Well, I know! He took Fisher's pin away from her and said he was going to send it back to the follow. And then Geraldine threw his own pin back at him and chucked herself down on the floor in hysterics and said she never wanted to see him or his pin again. She'd rather have kind Mr. Fisher. Then Hemingway saw red and stuck the pin — his own pin — in her back and killed her."

"That's more like it," said Smart. "Then he lost his head and ran away, with the Broad Street pin in his hand and Fisher's pin in his pocket."

"Yes — yes. And then he realised what he was doing, and hid the Broad Street pin where Johnson afterwards found it."

"Splendid!" cried Smart. "It all fits in. Then the next thing he hears is that Fisher has found Geraldine's body and is suspected of the murder. Nothing could be handier for him. But then, on Monday night the telephone message came through from Johnson mentioning the Broad Street pin."

Oliver smacked his hand on the table.

"Of course," he cried, "and now I understand one thing that always puzzled me. *That*'s why Hemingway took Johnson's message down himself over the 'phone instead of getting the verbatim man to do it in the ordinary way. He was altering Broad Street to Bond Street, to incriminate Fisher. And *that*'s why he made all that fuss about getting Johnson up to town with his story, instead of having the whole thing taken down at once and sent down to the printers properly."

"I dare say you're right," said the Inspector. "Well, then, I take it Hemingway must have prepared his plot before he left the office. He went off home and fetched the Bond Street pin – Fisher's pin – and wrote his 'Out of Order' notice for the call-box and went down to meet Johnson's train at Victoria. What would he do when he got there?"

"He'd ask to see the stuff," replied Oliver – "Johnson's story and the weapon and so on. Then he'd get him into the call-box –"

"What for?" asked Smart.

"He'd suggest ringing up the shop in Broad Street to see if they could identify the pin. He'd push Johnson in first, and then – biff! One good blow, and there's an end of Johnson and his evidence. And he uses – not the Broad Street pin, but the Bond Street pin – Fisher's pin – and he leaves it there, all nicely blood-stained, in a not *too*-conspicuous position – all ready to be found and to clinch Fisher's guilt. And so it very well might have done; if only Miss Blackwood hadn't listened in on that message. . . . I say, though," Oliver broke off, "I thought Hemingway had an alibi for the Victoria part of the business."

"So did I," answered Smart grimly, "but he hasn't." And he told Oliver the story of the faked time signal.

"That's fine," said Oliver. "That's great! Excuse me, I'll have to get this off to the *Courier* while it's hot. I–"

"You can't do that, Mr. Oliver. I'm going to get Gladys Sharp up from the Jumbles, and if she identifies Hemingway as Tracey, we shall arrest him this afternoon."

Hemingway, returning to the *Morning Star* offices after lunch, glanced, as had now become his habit, at the group of idlers near the gap in the hoardings. There was always a group of idlers at that point, watching the demolition of the old *Morning Star* offices to make way for the grander and more palatial building which was to be erected on the same site. Yes – the man was still there. A big, hefty fellow. Hemingway had noticed him lounging about there for the last two days – in fact, ever since Redman's name had been mentioned in connection with the attack on Beryl Blackwood. A very persistent idler.

As he entered the office by the front door, he observed another man whose bulky figure seemed familiar – a street hawker, with a barrow full of apples.

Hemingway frowned, He hoped all this vigilance was meant for Redman, but he had an unpleasant sensation of being watched all the morning, both at his house in Hampstead and on his way up in the Tube.

He took the lift up to his room, but, instead of getting on with his work, found himself idling and dreaming in a way very unlike himself. That man Smart had been up at the house again, asking questions. Fortunately, that alibi of his for the night of Johnson's murder was absolutely foolproof. But there were other things.

His hand stole to his breast-pocket. There was one precaution he ought to have taken — something he ought to have got rid of. But where — and how? He looked round the room. The subeditor was there, grunting over some galley-slips. There was extraordinarily little privacy in a newspaper office. And no place was safe up at Hampstead. For all he knew, the police were already there with a search-warrant.

The telephone rang. Two steamers had collided in mid-Channel. What else could one expect in this foggy weather? He made his decisions and gave his orders mechanically.

The afternoon seemed to drag on interminably. A cup of tea was brought him and he drank it greedily. A difficulty arose about page nine. In wrestling with it, he almost forgot his anxieties, and when the telephone rang again he answered it without foreboding.

"Inspector Smart would like a word with you, Sir."

Hemingway gulped.

"Send him up."

The sub-editor glanced up interrogatively.

"Yes," said Hemingway, with dry lips. "You'd better go, Perkins. And say we're not to be disturbed."

The young man went out by the glass door leading to the outer office. Hemingway glanced behind him to where there was a small second door – locked now, because it led to the old offices which were in process of demolition. He stepped swiftly across, unlocked it and transferred the key to the outer side.

The glass door opened, to admit Inspector Smart and somebody else, half-hidden behind him.

"Hullo, Inspector!" said Hemingway, genially. "This *is* an unexpected pleasure."

"Good afternoon, Sir," replied Smart. He moved aside a little, bringing his companion into view.

"Why, 'ullo!" said the latter. "Why – if it isn't – no, it ain't – yes it is – lor' now, it's Mr. Tracey. I didn't 'ardly recognise you with your moustache turned up so smart."

Hemingway rose, his hand fumbling in his breast, and took a few swift steps back from the desk.

"It's no good, Sir," said Smart. "Best come quiet. Jumbles murder, Mr. Hemingway, and the Victoria business as well. We've looked into that time-signal. . . . Ah! would you!"

They leapt for the little door together. Hemingway's hand shot out – there was a flash of steel and a yelp of pain. Then he was through, slamming the door and locking it upon Smart, who, with the blood streaming from him, was blowing his whistle and setting his uninjured shoulder to the lock.

Hemingway ran.

Along the deserted corridors, up and down stairs, twisting this way and that. A distant crash behind him told him that the door was down. But he could make it yet. The iron staircase down to the old composing room. Out and across the excavations. Surely he could dodge them there.

He ran — past the rows of empty offices, through the old news-room, and down the familiar passage and out through the door to the iron staircase. Panting, he flung the door open — and checked — gaping — staggering on the edge of space.

The staircase — the whole block was gone; pulled down — vanished in a day. The roar of London came up about him through the thick air. A great derrick swung over his head. Far down, two hundred feet below, workmen toiled among the fallen brickwork.

There was a shout behind him. Feet pounded down the corridor. He sprang desperately out upon the scaffolding. A whistle blew urgently, and the man in charge of the derrick on its high gantry turned, looked up and began to swarm hurriedly up a ladder towards him.

No chance that way. He turned, snarling, to face pursuit, and, in turning, slipped on the greasy plank. His hands clutched the air for an endless moment. Then the world swung over like a spinning wheel as the earth rushed up to meet him.

* * *

As Inspector Smart, his shoulder hurriedly bandaged with an office towel, bent over the body, he found Oliver beside him.

"Damnation!" said the Inspector. "There's my whole case gone west. And just as we got the last bit of evidence, too!" He held out his hand. On it lay a long, thin dagger – an oriental pin with the head of a goddess carved in green jade.

"Yes," said Oliver. He glanced shudderingly at the smashed and pitiful body. Then the master instinct reasserted itself. "Yes, but – by God! I can publish my story now!"

The head printer of the *Daily Courier* stood up in the high gallery, looking down on the machines. The outer pages, still hot from the foundry, had been lifted from the cylinders, clamped into place, made ready. It was eleven o'clock. He raised his hand to the switch.

"Ready down there?" "Ready." "Let her go."

The switch clicked down. With a steady and increasing roar the machines sprang to life. The paper reeled out under the rollers. The tall building shivered, throbbed, shuddered into one long thunder of reverberation. Rumbling and clanking, thousand after thousand, the *Couriers* sped forth to tell an eager world of a Fleet Street editor's crimes and crash to death. All over the building, men rubbed their hands and chuckled.

"It's a scoop for the *Courier* all right," they said. "By God! What a wonderful scoop!"

BEHIND THE SCREEN

hugh walpole, agatha christie, dorothy l. sayers, anthony berkeley, e. c. bentley, and ronald knox

I

by hugh walpole

Hate was the principal feeling in young Wilfred Hope's mind as he walked hurriedly down Sunflower Lane one wet and stormy evening. Hatred was not his natural emotion. Indeed, until a year ago he had been a clever, bright, happy young student at one of the larger London hospitals with splendid prospects of a fine career, and his only thoughts had been for his work and for the girl to whom he was engaged, whom he loved more than his work or life itself. Life had been everything that was happy and industrious and gay, and now, as he hurried along, it was everything that was sinister and troubled and foreboding. He had for many months now spent evening after evening after supper in the comfortable, cosy home of the Ellises, the family to which Amy Ellis, the girl to whom he was engaged, belonged. And, as he hurried along to the Ellises' house, in spite of his agitation and disturbance, and even, perhaps, something — for who knows exactly what was in his heart — even perhaps something of terror, he was thinking to himself how desperately things lately had changed, and

changed, as he well knew, entirely because of
one person, and it was this person who was dom-
inating his mind so especially.

Almost exactly a year before this evening the
Ellises had taken, as a kind of paying guest, a
man, Paul Dudden. Dudden was some forty-five
years of age, heavy, stout, white-faced, unattrac-
tive, monosyllabic; engaged, it seemed, in some
business in the City, but he had offered the Ellises, who were none too well off, some considerable income for his sojourn, so they had taken
him eagerly as their guest. They had taken him
in the greatest innocence of their hearts, but
within a very short period Dudden, who had
seemed at first a man of no particular personality,
had acquired over all of them a most curious dom-
inance. Young Wilfred thought of the family —
stout, good-natured Mrs. Ellis, with her cheerful
smile and her easy, happy way of taking things;
old Mr. Ellis, very much older than his wife, a
little shrimp of a man; young Robert, a boy of,
perhaps, twenty or so, not very prepossessing,
rather of the pimply, pale, uneasy order at present, showing no very great disposition to work,
rather a worry to his parents; and the fourth of
the family, Amy herself, who was, as young
Wilfred thought, the loveliest of all the girls in
England — and, indeed, without his own particular prejudice, she was a girl of extraordinary
charm. This was the Ellis family, and within a
short period of Dudden coming to them they had
begun most mysteriously to change. Old Mr.
Ellis, who had always been a nervous, shy little
man, had seemed to redouble his shyness and
uneasiness. Amy herself had lost some of her

brightness. Young Robert was more sullen, more silent than he had been. Only cheerful Mrs. Ellis seemed to show no change. As for Wilfred, who can describe the change in his heart? As he walked, the thin rain beating in his face, the wind tearing among the trees on either side, the storm seemed to portray some of his own hideous feeling. For it was hideous. He who had never, perhaps, in all his life disliked anyone, now wished every evil possible to this man; for not only did he threaten the peace and happiness of the family for which Wilfred cared most in the world, but also it seemed that of late he had been having a strange influence over Amy herself; and Wilfred had even a kind of fear that she might break off her engagement with him. So, indeed, he was a miserable creature as he hastened.

He reached the little gate, pushed it back, hurried up the little garden path, rang the bell on the so familiar door. For a moment he had a strange disposition to return. Something seemed to say to him that tonight he would be better away. He had felt it on several occasions of late; the evenings had not been the sort of happy ones they used to be. But no, his pride refused to keep him back; he rang the bell and waited. The door was almost at once opened by a very familiar figure – the large-capped housekeeper, friend, servant of the family, Mrs. Hulk, a woman who had been with the Ellises for many years. Wilfred usually stayed and spoke with her, for he was a great favourite of hers, but tonight in his own agitation and unhappiness he brushed past her just nodding, and hurried into the stuffy little hall. He hurried, indeed, so fast that he did not notice that after he had gone Mrs. Hulk, not closing the door, stepped outside into the wind and the rain – stepped outside, hurried down the little path, and stood by the gate looking eagerly up and down the little road. That was indeed unusual behaviour for her, for she was a most placid and happy person, but tonight her large, broad face was wrinkled with anxiety as she looked about her. Was she expecting someone? Did she fancy that someone was hiding behind those dark, whirling trees? Was it, perhaps, that she was waiting for a message or a sign? At any rate, there in the wind and the rain she stood, so absorbed in her own particular purpose that she never noticed what was going on around her. Wilfred meanwhile had hung up his hat, put away his coat, and knocked on the familiar door, entering without waiting, and there saw the scene to which he was so accustomed.

The drawing-room of the Ellises was of the old-fashioned kind, the last word, perhaps, in comfort, because the furniture had been used by them all for so long, but by our modern ideas desperately overcrowded – little tables covered with photographs and knick-knacks, and on the mantelpiece above the roaring fire strange Chinese ornaments, dogs with blue faces, mandarins and their ladies, and large vases with "everlastings" brushing a little dustily one against the other. And, covering almost all the farther end of one wall, stood a large old-fashioned Japanese screen, which was to Wilfred by now almost as familiar as his own clothes; a screen covered with black and gilt figures of a familiar kind, and near it a large pot with an aspidistra. Mrs. Ellis was sitting by the fire reading, as she loved to do, out of a novel, aloud. Opposite her was Amy, who gave Wilfred a smile as he came in. Near her, moving uneasily in his chair, sat young Robert; and at a little table not far away was old Mr. Ellis, bent up over the table playing his favourite game of Patience, as was always his evening custom.

Wilfred sat down opposite the screen and near Mrs. Ellis. She was reading "'Oh!'" she read, "'Oh, Robert!' cried Lucy, 'Mine at last! How long I have waited for this moment.' And hurrying across the floor he threw himself on his knees before his beloved, clasping her in his arms."

"There," cried Mrs. Ellis, for a moment letting the book drop into her lap. "Isn't that perfectly beautiful?" Amy nodded, to please her mother. Wilfred indeed did not hear the words, for, strangely, from the moment that he had entered and sat down, he felt an uneasiness quite new in his experience. Was it his own disturbed feelings or was there really something in the room? He sat there telling himself not to be foolish; but no, the impression grew. There were all the familiar things, the little tables, the photographs, the china ornaments, the screen, everything so comfortable, the roaring fire, the family he knew so well; but he had the oddest impression that somewhere, behind the curtain, behind the screen, even behind himself — and this was the most awful fear of all — some other person was also in the room, shadowing him, standing over him, watching his every movement.

His discomfort grew. Mrs. Ellis's voice seemed to whirl in the air with a strange, indeterminate

sound. He could not listen to her voice. He
looked at Amy to reassure himself, and then,
oddly, although he loved her so much, he had a
fear lest she should look up and meet his eyes.
He did not want to meet them, but this sense that
he was himself in a way a criminal made him even
more uneasy than before. His gaze wandered to
young Robert, tall, thin and bony, with clothes
that fitted him not too well, sitting awkwardly in
his chair, jerking himself backwards and for-
wards; and as he jerked himself Wilfred was suddenly aware that his white cuffs shot out with
each jerk from beyond his sleeves. These cuffs
fascinated Wilfred and, looking more closely, he
suddenly seemed to see on them some strange
markings. Could they be stains? Ink, perhaps. No.
Something. He tried to look more closely, but the
room began to swim, possibly with the heat of the
fire – and then he fancied that young Robert was
aware of his glance and shot his cuffs back again,
and even put one hand over one of them to stop
its protruding. Were there marks on those cuffs?
Was there something that Robert wanted to hide?
And then he began inwardly to laugh at his own
sense of disturbance. What could be quieter and
more happy now than this room, with his friends,
everything, with the old clock ticking the minutes
away? His agitation continued. He began himself
to be desperately restless. He moved his chair a
little, and so came closer to old Mr. Ellis, bent
up over the table, playing with cards. He
watched, trying to get rid of his own irritation,
and as he watched he was suddenly aware of the
strangest thing. For old Mr. Ellis – so shy and
nervous and ordinary a little man, who had never,

surely, done anything wrong in the whole of his life, who was dominated almost completely by his charming, happy and merry wife – old Mr. Ellis was not playing Patience, although he was moving the cards. One fell upon another in the little rows that belonged to the game, but they fell in complete disorder; there was no discipline of numbers or of colours; he was moving them idly, his thoughts far away. What was the matter? Of what was he thinking? Why was he not playing? And Wilfred tried to see if he could discover in him some special anxiety. But his face was hidden, and while he watched, now becoming so convinced that somebody else was indeed in the room beside himself, he almost burst out, interrupting the reading with, "Tell me, is Dudden coming in tonight?" – although he knew that it was a fatal question to ask, for at the name of that heavy, sinister, stout, pale-faced man all the Ellis family seemed at once to change their nature, to shrink inside themselves, to guard themselves against some enemy. And so feeling, and so conscious that whatever else he did the name of Dudden must never be mentioned, but wanting with a kind of burning anxiety to turn direct to Amy and say, "Well, what's that man been saying to you today, dear?" – knowing that that would blow the whole family, as it were, into the air like an explosion, holding himself in with the most desperate intention, so he sat, and in spite of his intention knew that he was waiting for something.

He wished, if he could, to get nearer to young Robert. He had such a strange suspicion that the boy was desperately unhappy, and although he had never liked him and they had nothing in common, still he felt that perhaps he could explain something of the distress that he was suffering. He moved his chair yet again and, as he moved it, he was conscious he was now very close to cheerful Mrs. Ellis. He was conscious that the whole room seemed to change its position. So fantastic now were his fears and agitations that it seemed to him as though every piece of furniture there – yes, and every small piece of china, every little photograph, every little family album – were all playing some part, that they had a consciousness of somebody's presence there beyond his own. It was as though he would have liked to have picked up those china ornaments and asked them to say whether they could give him some of their secret.

This was absurd. He had not been so clever a medical student for so long, he had not experienced so many strange, direct, real things in life that he could not now control himself. So in his determination that he would show no emotion, that he would beat down his own agitation, he moved his chair again. And now he suddenly realised that he could see – behind the screen. He looked, and at that sight suddenly his whole being seemed to be convulsed with a dreadful terror. Now, indeed, there was reason enough. He gripped the arms of his chair. The whole room swam up like the surging deck of a ship in a stormy sea and surged down again, and he could hear all the little china ornaments and the tables and the albums re-settle themselves with a kind of sigh. For behind the screen, lying there huddled up, almost as though in sleep, his dreadful head turned towards Wilfred, pale, ashen, lying upon an arm, his heavy body crumpled up in a kind of strange attitude as though someone had twisted its limbs in different directions, there, dead beyond any question, lay Dudden. Dudden dead, and Dudden horribly dead. For now Wilfred saw in his exceeding horror that from the collar, and the neck that protruded, spread a thin stream of most dreadful blood, staining the carpet, spreading farther and farther, welling out in the most dreadful, uninterrupted sequence. He saw with a new terror that the stream would soon be beyond the screen. Soon the others in the room would see it. Soon his horror would be theirs. He was about to cry. He saw it lying heavily, spread out, and now, as it seemed, entrapping with its sinister signs the whole room. Mrs. Ellis, with a sigh of satisfaction at the beauty of what she was reading, once more let the book drop, looked up smiling at the company, looked up and saw that dreadful stream, looked up and gave a shrill cry – "Look! look! the blood!"

II

by agatha christie

With Mrs. Ellis's shriek, Wilfred regained possession of his faculties. The numbing feeling of paralysis passed away. He was himself once more, cool, efficient, able to take command of the situation.

Crossing the room, he knelt by Dudden's body. He was vaguely aware of the others; of Mr. Ellis, half risen from the card table, his mouth open, his eyes staring; of Amy, of Robert, of Mrs. Ellis. They were all there behind him, waiting, peering, listening for the authoritative words he would soon speak.

He was careful not in any way to disturb the position of the body – a queer huddled position – he noted it automatically. The most cursory examination was all that was needed. Dudden was dead. The blood had welled from a wound in the neck, near the angle of the jawbone.

There was a curious expression on Wilfred's face as he bent over the dead man. Those eyes – those dead staring eyes – why surely. . . ? No, this wasn't his business. He mustn't imagine things. But it was odd – distinctly odd.

He rose to his feet. . . .

"He's dead," he said briefly.

"Oh!" It was a low moaning cry that broke from Amy's lips. She turned deathly pale, swayed, and clutched at her mother.

"Come, my dear, come." The stout woman was compelling. "Come, Amy love. . . ."

Putting her arm round the girl, she led her gently from the room. Her supporting arm kept the girl from falling.

Wilfred drew a sigh of relief as the women left the room. His eyes met those of Mr. Ellis. The latter seemed to be recovering from the shock.

"This is terrible – terrible," he ejaculated. "What is it, my boy? Suicide, I suppose. A terrible thing to happen in one's house."

"It's not suicide," said Wilfred.

"Not suicide – eh?"

"I'm not saying the wound couldn't have been self-inflicted. It could, though it's very unlikely. But in that case the weapon would have been still in the wound."

"The weapon?"

"Yes. He's been stabbed – stabbed with a sharp, narrow blade and there's no sign of such a thing anywhere near him. This is a case for the police, Mr. Ellis."

"You mean –"

"This is murder!" He repeated the word: "*Murder*. . . ."

"Murder? You can't mean it?"

"There's no doubt of it. You must ring up the police at once."

"I – I –"

Mr. Ellis hesitated, swallowed nervously, then went shakily from the room.

Really, Wilfred supposed, he ought to have offered to telephone for him. The old man was so upset that he hardly knew what he was doing, whereas he, Wilfred, was perfectly calm and collected. Nevertheless, he had felt the strongest objection to leaving the room. His place was here.

His attention was suddenly drawn to Robert. The young man was standing by the edge of the screen. He was staring downwards with fascinated eyes. Wilfred could see the Adam's apple in his throat jerking up and down, while his long pale fingers twisted and untwisted themselves nervously. A thoroughly neurotic type, Wilfred thought rather disgustedly.

How strangely the boy was staring at Dudden. No – that was odd – he was not looking at Dudden at all. His fascinated gaze was elsewhere – on the tiny rivulet of blood. It seemed to fascinate him. He looked almost hypnotised. Suddenly, with a convulsive shudder, Robert seemed to come to himself. He turned abruptly and almost ran from the room.

Wilfred felt a sense of relief. He was alone. Once more, he bent over the body, examining it carefully. Curious attitude – the man might have been asleep, but for that tell-tale stream of scarlet. And his eyes — most peculiar! An unpleasant man, given to unpleasant vices, but all the same Wilfred had never noticed before – Oh! well, why think of it?

He raised a hand to brush the hair from his forehead and then started nervously.

There was blood on his fingers!

How did it come there? He had been most careful in his handling of Dudden. He had not touched the wound. He bent lower. There were dark smears on the cloth of Dudden's coat near its lower edge. He touched them – yes, they were faintly damp. They were smears of blood. How had they got there?

A slight sound made him turn his head. For a moment he saw nothing. The room was the same as usual – almost indecently peaceful. The patience cards still laid out on the table, Mrs. Ellis's book, a paper cutter between its pages, lying on her chair, a silk scarf of Amy's lying on the arm of the sofa. It was all as usual, as he had seen it a hundred times before.

The sound was repeated and now Wilfred recognised it for what it was. Someone was pushing the door very cautiously open. He waited. Suddenly the rubicund face of Mrs. Hulk came peering round the door; an expression of mingled fear and excitement animated her countenance. She seemed taken aback at the sight of Wilfred. Then she pushed the door a little further and came in. Her hands fingered her apron.

"'E's dead, is 'e?" she asked, in a hoarse voice.

Wilfred nodded. He had just time to note that an expression of distinct satisfaction passed over her face when the doorbell rang. Mrs. Hulk went to answer it. There was a murmur of voices and Wilfred heard her say: "'E's in there. The young gentleman's there, too." Two men entered the room. The first wore the uniform of a police inspector, the second Wilfred put down correctly as the police surgeon.

"Evening," said the Inspector. "Are you Mr. Ellis?"

"No — my name is Hope."

He explained the circumstances, indicated the body (which the Inspector viewed without any show of emotion) and suggested that he should fetch Mr. Ellis.

"That's right," said the Inspector. "But don't leave the house, Mr. Hope. I shall want a word with you presently. All right, Dr. Larkin, you go ahead."

Wilfred left the room. The door from the hall to the kitchen was open and he had a glimpse of Mrs. Ellis calmly and methodically helping Mrs. Hulk to wash up the supper dishes.

"Is that you, Wilfred?" she called. "Mrs. Hulk tells me the police have come."

"Yes. They want Mr. Ellis."

"I think he's in the dining-room."

She finished wiping a coffee cup, hung the glass-cloth neatly on its nail and joined Wilfred in the hall.

"How is Amy?"

"She is lying down on her bed, poor child. I have given her some sal volatile. She was completely overcome. It was, of course, a terrible shock for a young girl. And Amy is particularly sensitive. The police will not want to see her, will they?"

"I should not think so."

"Here's Father," said Mrs. Ellis, opening the dining-room door.

Mr. Ellis was sitting on a chair by the window. His face was buried in his hands. He started up nervously as they entered.

"What — I — what —"

"The police, dear," said his wife. "They've come."

"Oh! yes — yes, of course. They'll want to — to know about things — eh? I wonder what sort of things — eh?"

"They'll ask, of course, when you last saw Dudden alive," said Wilfred. "When did you, by the way?"

"At supper," said Mrs. Ellis. "We were late tonight — Father was late home."

"We were still at table when he left the house," said Mr. Ellis.

"Left the house?"

"Yes. Yes. He got up and went out rather abruptly. He fairly banged the front door after him. Something odd about him tonight, don't you think so, my dear?"

"One's always inclined to think that after a thing's happened," said Mrs. Ellis.

"What time did he go out?" asked Wilfred.

"I'm not quite sure. It must have been about a quarter past nine."

"And you never saw him again," said Wilfred slowly. "You don't know when he returned to the house?"

Mrs. Ellis shook her head.

"And the rest of you — what did you do?"

"Well — we sat here round the table a bit longer — ten minutes maybe — and then we went into the parlour."

"And none of you left the room during that ten minutes?"

"We were all here," answered Mrs. Ellis quickly. "Father — you'd better be going along.

The police are waiting."

Mr. Ellis hurried quickly from the room. Wilfred wondered whether it was his fancy or whether he had been right in thinking that a slight expression of astonishment had passed over the old man's face at the last words his wife had spoken.

Would he have given a different answer?

"I suppose Mrs. Hulk would know when Dudden returned to the house?" Wilfred remarked.

"Possibly, but he had his own latchkey, you know. He never needed to ring the bell."

"I might ask her at any rate."

Mrs. Ellis raised no objection, and Wilfred left the room meaning to question Mrs. Hulk forthwith. But as he passed through the hall his purpose was diverted by a neat staccato rat-a-tat-tat on the front door. Wilfred opened the door. Outside he was confronted by someone whom he always thought of to himself as "That little mottled man from next door." So Mrs. Ellis had once described Mr. Parsons, the owner of "Swallowcliffe," and the description remained in Wilfred's mind.

Excitement had caused Mr. Parsons to look more mottled than ever. He was stammering with pleasurable excitement.

"Excuse me," he said. "Excuse me. But is it really true that there has been murder done? I heard it on good authority, but could hardly believe my ears."

"It's quite true," said Wilfred curtly. He was strongly disposed to shut the door in his questioner's face.

"Mr. Dudden, so I was told?"

"Yes."

This time Wilfred did begin to close the door, but Mr. Parsons took an eager step forward and placed himself in the aperture.

"You must pardon this seeming intrusion. But I have information to give — valuable information. Indeed it is so."

"What information?"

"I saw the murderer — I am convinced I saw the murderer. Twenty minutes past nine — I remember the time precisely. I was looking out of my study window. A great hulking ruffian of a man — possibly — I cannot be sure on this point — but possibly the worse for drink. He came through the front gate and slunk round the house towards the back in what I can only call a highly suspicious manner. Ten minutes later he reappeared and slunk out — positively slunk out. Oh! a highly suspicious character — known to the police, I do not doubt. Possibly a member of a gang."

Wilfred wondered for a moment whether the whole story was a fabrication, but Mr. Parsons' earnestness convinced him.

"Well," he said, "I'll mention it to the Inspector. Thank you very much."

"Not at all. It was my duty."

"Quite so. By the way, Mr. Dudden went out at a quarter past nine. Did you happen to see his return?"

"No, I did not. I did not see him go out either. Mr. Dudden has neither left the house nor returned to it this evening, I am sure of that. My study window, you know."

"You may not have noticed."

Mr. Parsons positively squeaked with indignation.

"I notice everything – everything! Nothing escapes me. I have trained myself to observe. Yes, I can assure you, I notice everything. I even noticed the light in the bathroom – most unusual at such an early hour."

"I beg your pardon," said Wilfred, soothingly. "Most remarkable and er – painstaking. Thank you very much. I'll tell the Ellises."

"If I could be of any assistance," said Mr. Parsons eagerly.

"Oh thanks," said Wilfred. "But I don't think there's anything. The police, you know, they're in charge and all that."

He managed at last to shut the door.

He was somewhat startled by what Mr. Parsons had told him. After a moment's reflection, he went into the kitchen. Mrs. Hulk was alone there.

He began by asking her whether she knew at what hour Dudden had returned. Her answer was given tartly.

"I don't know. How should I? Got 'is key, 'e 'ad."

"He did go out, I suppose?"

"Of course he went out. Slammed the door fit to shake the 'ouse. In a temper, if you arsk me. 'E'd a narsty temper. I've seen it more than once."

"Has anyone been to the house this evening?"

"What d'yer mean, been to the 'ouse?"

"Well, it seems a man was seen coming round to the back door – a great hulking brute, I understand."

Mrs. Hulk turned very red.

"What d'you mean with yer narsty puns?"

"Puns? I don't understand you."

"Yer said 'hulking' didn't yer? Oh! yes, it was Hulk right enough. Cadging round as usual. Half my week's wages, I 'ad to give him, before he'd take 'imself off. A bit the worse, 'e was. And that's not unusual."

Wilfred soothed her by assuring her that no pun had been meant. That matter seemed cleared up satisfactorily.

Suddenly remembering Parsons' remark about the bathroom, on an impulse he ran up the stairs. The bathroom was situated just at the angle of the stairs. He pushed the door open and entered. There was nothing luxuriant or magnificent about the bathroom. It was small and rather dirty looking. The varnished paper was peeling off in one corner. Wilfred looked about him. Nothing here. Indeed, what should there be? He was just turning to depart when he noticed some dark spots on the linoleum in front of the wash-basin. He stooped, scrutinized them, then he touched one gingerly with his finger. His face grew rather white. *The spots on the floor were spots of blood.* . . . A voice spoke from the doorway. It was Mrs. Hulk. "You're wanted in the parlour." Wilfred descended the stairs mechanically, his mind busy. In the parlour the Inspector was seated at a table. The doctor was standing near the window.

"Now, Mr. Hope, I should like a few words from you."

"Certainly. I don't know, though, that I can add very much to what you know already."

"We've had a full account from Mr. Ellis. It's not that so much. But there are one or two minor points where I think you may be able to assist us."

"Of course, if I can, I shall be only too glad."

"Thank you. For instance – this case –" He produced it suddenly, rather like a conjuror. "You recognise it – eh?"

"I – well, yes, of course, it's mine."

"A case of surgical instruments?"

"Yes."

"You brought it here – when?"

"Yesterday, I think. I must have forgotten it."

"Just so. Was it complete? Anything lost or missing from it?"

Wilfred stared at him in surprise.

"Certainly it was complete. It's practically brand new."

"Nothing was missing? You're sure?"

"Quite sure."

"And yet – something *is* missing." The Inspector opened the case. *"One of the surgical knives is missing, Mr. Hope."*

Startled, Wilfred met the Inspector's gaze fixed full upon him. What was there behind that glance? Was it – suspicion?

A feeling of deadly sickness surged over him.

III

by dorothy l. sayers

"A surgical knife missing?" stammered Wilfred. "Are – are you sure?"

For answer the Inspector held out the case, open, showing the rows of shining steel instruments, each held neatly in place by a little leather girdle. There was a collection of scalpels, ranged side by side like needles in a needle-case. The central one of the row was undoubtedly gone.

"Oh, *that* –" said Wilfred, as airily as he could. "*That* knife. Oh, yes, I see. Well, now that I come to look at it I can't be *absolutely* sure about it, I know I have got the knife *somewhere* – it is not missing in that sense. But I could not swear that I did not leave it in the dissecting-room. Or the man I dig with may have borrowed it. He is a terror for borrowing things. Er – I will have a hunt for it when I get home."

"Thank you, sir. That would be a great assistance. We do not want to waste time looking for a mare's nest, you know." Inspector Rice laughed cheerily, but to Wilfred the mirth had an ominous and sarcastic sound.

"Now, Mr. Hope, I understand you were the first person to examine the body, and you gave it as your opinion that he had been murdered. Yes. What made you so certain of that, Mr. Hope? The wound is in quite a possible position for suicide, you see. It is not as though he had been stabbed in the middle of the back, for instance."

"Of course not," replied Wilfred, conscious that the police-surgeon was eyeing him with what seemed to him diabolical amusement. "Perhaps I spoke rather impulsively. The – er – direction of the stab, and the fact that there was no weapon to be seen – I think that was what was in my mind."

"That was all, was it? You had no reason for supposing that anybody might have a motive for murdering this Mr. – er – this Mr. Dudden?"

"Good Lord, no!" said Wilfred, hastily.

"You, yourself, were on friendly terms with him?"

"I did not know him frightfully well," explained Wilfred. "We met as – as friendly acquaintances, you know."

"Just so. And you knew of no little differences between him and the household?"

Wilfred wondered very much what Mr. Ellis had been saying, but replied, with more truth to the letter than to the spirit, "I never saw or heard anything pass of an unfriendly nature."

"Just so, just so," said the Inspector. "All friends together. You are engaged to Miss Ellis, I believe?"

"Yes, I am," said Wilfred, a little defiantly.

"Ah, h'm. This must have been a sad shock to

the young lady. Do you happen to know, sir, what were Mr. Dudden's feeling towards Miss Ellis?"

The question was slipped in so sharply and shrewdly that it nearly threw Wilfred off his guard. He took refuge in an embarrassed laugh.

"His feelings? Come now, Inspector, he would not be likely to confide his feelings to *me*, would he? No doubt he admired Miss Ellis. I think everybody admires her."

"I am quite sure of that, sir," said the Inspector, with cast-iron gravity. "Well, now, Mr. Hope, you told Mr. Ellis that everything must be left just as it was, and the police sent for? That was very right and proper. Mr. Ellis sent the telephone message, I think? Yes. Can you tell us where the rest of the family were at that time?"

"Miss Ellis felt unwell," said Wilfred, "and Mrs. Ellis took her upstairs. Robert stayed here with me."

"All the time?"

"No, not all the time. He went out. I do not know where he went."

"Did anybody else come in?"

"Mrs. Hulk, the cook, looked in for a moment, just before you came. She went out again to let you in."

"I see. First you and Mr. Robert – then you by yourself – then you and Mrs. Hulk. We were round in about ten minutes after getting the message, I think, Doctor? – or say, a quarter of an hour. You would have been alone with the body for five or six minutes, then, Mr. Hope?"

"About that," agreed Wilfred. His tongue seemed dry and the words did not come out very well. "I was the most suitable person to stay with it," he added. "I am a medical student, you see. A dead body is not so shocking to me as to other people."

"Exactly so, sir. Did you make any search for the weapon during these five or six minutes?"

"No. None. I just stood by. I touched nothing."

"I wish everybody showed as much common-sense," said the Inspector, heartily. "Now, as regards the earlier part of the evening? You arrived about ten o'clock?"

"Yes. I was shown straight in here. The whole family was here together, and I am quite certain that nobody left their seat even for a moment until the body was discovered. Mrs. Ellis was reading—"

The Inspector interrupted him.

"Just a moment." His eye had wandered to the doorway. "Who is that, please? Do you want anybody?"

A small figure came forward into the light, and Wilfred, with a sense of irritation, recognised the persistent Mr. Parsons.

"Oh, I *do* beg your pardon, Inspector. I *hope* I'm not intruding. The front door was on the latch, so I just came in. I thought you might like to take my evidence yourself, though this young gentleman has doubtless told you all about it."

"He has not told us anything so far," said the Inspector, fixing a questioning eye on Wilfred.

"I was just going to, Inspector, only you didn't give me time," explained the young man, hurriedly. "Though, as a matter of fact, I went at once to Mrs. Hulk and asked about it, and she cleared the whole thing up, so I really thought it was hardly worth bothering you about."

"I think that's for me to judge, sir, if you don't mind." The Inspector turned to Mr. Parsons, who at once plunged happily and eagerly into his tale of the ruffian seen going round to the back door.

"H'm," said Inspector Rice, "it's a pity I didn't hear of this earlier!"

"Yes, but —" said Wilfred. He felt that he was making matters worse with every word, but he gave Mrs. Hulk's version of the matter, and went on:

"After all, Inspector, I don't see that that could have had anything to do with it. The man was out of the house at half past nine, and if Dudden had been killed as early as that the blood would have coagulated long before 10:25, when I saw it still trickling from behind the screen. Of course, this linoleum surround is waxed, and the floors uneven, which would help the blood to travel, and the room was very hot. Still, the floor is the coldest part of it, and you would expect the blood to clot in about fifteen minutes or so — that is to say —" He stopped, realising rather too late where this display of medical science was leading him.

"Quite so," said the Inspector, with the air of one triumphantly snapping the spring of a trap, "but don't you see, sir, that that would bring the time of the death to ten past ten. Now you tell me that you and all the family were here in this room from ten o'clock till 10:25. How would you explain that?"

"Yes, I see," said Wilfred, unhappily. "Well, I can't explain it. It must have been earlier — of course it must."

Dr. Larkin smiled.

"In any case," he said, "there is no need to assume that the man died immediately after the stabbing. A constant flow of warm blood would help to retard the clotting."

"Of course it would," said Wilfred. The trap was not a real trap at all; it was a bluff. He reflected savagely that at least the Inspector had gained nothing by it.

Mr. Parsons, meanwhile, was gazing at the body with frank interest.

"Dear, dear," he squeaked, "how very strange it seems. So large a man, and so small a wound — and yet it killed him — yes, yes. Death hath so many doors to let out life, as the poet observes. Not as wide as a church-door, but 'tis enough, 'twill serve. Shakespeare, you know. And no sign of any struggle. They thought him dying when he slept, and sleeping when he died. I forget who wrote that. Yes. Such a curious place for him to be in, isn't it? But he wasn't put there — he was sitting or standing there when he was stabbed, and just toppled right over — you can see that by the way the blood has run straight down without smearing. Really, I am quite a Sherlock Holmes, am I not? I suppose this splash on the screen was made when the blood first gushed out. What a pity! It has run through underneath and stained the nice carpet! I wonder why he was hiding behind the screen?"

"That's what we don't know yet," said the Inspector.

"If he didn't die at once," said the little man, "why didn't he call out or try to crawl away? You *will* forgive my inquisitiveness, but it is all so interesting to me. I am such an observer. Nothing human is foreign to me, as Horace says — I think it is Horace, isn't it? Well, well, well. He must have fallen asleep, don't you think, Inspector? And slept very, very soundly."

The Inspector and the Doctor exchanged glances, and Wilfred wondered whether they, too, had noticed the strange contraction of the dead man's pupils.

"We shall know better about that," said Rice, "when we find out exactly when and how he got here."

"Well, now, I can help you there, Inspector," cried Mr. Parsons in great excitement. "Dear me, I'm so glad I came along — I can be quite useful to you after all. Now that I've seen the body lying just close under the window like this, I can tell you that it can't possibly have been there before 9:25. Wait — I'll tell you how I know, I happened to step out after dinner to put a letter in the pillar-box, just up the lane, and as I passed I noticed — I can't help noticing things — I noticed the lights go up in the room, and somebody drawing the curtains. I'm sure about the time, because I looked at my watch to see if I had caught the 9:30 post, and my watch is always right, because I set it by wireless time. So the poor fellow couldn't have been there at 9:25, or the person who drew the curtains would have noticed him, wouldn't they?"

"That may be important," said the Inspector. "Who drew the curtains?"

"That would be Mrs. Hulk, I think," said Wilfred. "Shall I fetch her?"

"No, thank you, sir," said the Inspector, civilly but firmly, "I think I'll go along and see her myself."

He marched away to the kitchen, leaving Mr.
Parsons to babble his questions to the doctor.
Wilfred followed him, but, on the way, ran into
Mrs. Ellis in the hall, and stopped to inquire after
Amy.

"Just fallen asleep, poor child," said her
mother. "She's simply stunned by the blow. It's
all come upon us so suddenly – I hardly know if
I'm on my head or my heels. What ought we to
do? Ought we to go into mourning? Mr. Dudden
was no relation, of course, and – and – nobody
liked him – but dying like this – in our house –
oh, dear! I have a new black frock just coming
home from the dressmaker's. Miss Pettigrew said
she would bring it round tonight. I thought I
might put it on, but I don't see it anywhere, do
you? Mrs. Hulk would know whether it came or
not. I must ask her."

"I don't think you'd better ask Mrs. Hulk just
now," said Wilfred. "The Inspector is interviewing her in the kitchen."

"Oh, dear, is he?" Mrs. Ellis clasped her
plump hands with a gesture almost of despair.
"What on earth can he want *her* for? Well, he
shan't come disturbing Amy. I won't have it. I'd
better go back to her."

She climbed the stairs heavily, with a new terror in her face.

In the meantime, Inspector Rice had elicited
from Mrs. Hulk the story of her husband's cadging visit to the house, and had passed on to his
second question.

"I can't rightly remember when I drawed the
curtains," said Mrs. Hulk thoughtfully. She
paused in her occupation of slicing beef for

the stock-pot, and rested the knife point downwards on the table, while she overhauled her memory. "It would be later than usual, owing to supper being put off. If the gentleman says it was five-and-twenty past, then I won't say any different."

"If Mr. Dudden had been sitting, or lying, behind the screen at the time, would you have noticed him?"

"Well, now —" Mrs. Hulk looked frankly into the Inspector's eyes — "that I couldn't say neither. I might, and then again, I might not. You see, when the light is on, it throws a heavy shadder be'ind that there screen, as you'll 'ave noticed for yourself."

"In point of fact, though, you did *not* see him?"

"No. No-o-o. No, I didn't *see* him." She considered again. "But come to think of it, I believe I did 'ear a sort of a 'eavy breathing, like. But I didn't pay no attention to that, puttin' it down to old Grip."

"Grip?"

"The bulldog," explained Mrs. Hulk. "'E often breathes 'eavy, on account of his nose bein' flat. Regular snorin', you'd call it."

"I see," said the Inspector, mentally noting that he would have to investigate Grip's movements as well as those of the family. "Very well, Mrs. Hulk. Now, where is this bathroom I've been hearing about?"

"Right at the top of the stairs, sir. You can't miss it. You can see the door from the 'all."

Mr. Parsons was already twittering upon the landing, and Wilfred had accompanied him upstairs, partly because he did not trust Mr. Parsons, and partly because he wanted to see what the Inspector would make of the bloodstains on the bathroom floor. But when the door was opened, he saw that they had come too late. The spots were gone. Not very long gone, either, for the floor bore traces of recent washing – a fact which did not escape the official eye.

"Looks as though someone had been wiping up something," said Inspector Rice. "Who did that?"

"Perhaps this gentleman could tell you," suggested Mr. Parsons, a trifle maliciously. "When I came in just now to see you, Inspector, I noticed him coming out of this door."

"This is monstrous," said Wilfred, feeling that if murders were going to be the fashion, he would gladly wring Mr. Parsons' scraggy neck. "I never touched the bathroom floor. I had nothing to do with it at all."

The Inspector said nothing. He was examining a little row of bottles above the fixed basin – aspirin tablets, tooth powder, health salts, ammoniated quinine and similar household trifles. Then a second door caught his attention. He opened it, disclosing a large cupboard, crammed with more bottles, boxes, boots, books, rugs, tins, discarded ornaments and picture-frames – in fact, a regular family "glory-hole." He rummaged about, grunting, for some time, and finally emerged with a small, flat, black-japanned case in his hands.

It was the kind of case that was issued to medical officers during the War, containing various kinds of drugs, many of them deadly, in small closely-stoppered glass tubes. Most of these appeared to be still intact. One of them, however, the Inspector held up. It was plainly labelled MORPHINE, and about half its contents were gone.

The Inspector's face was somewhat stern as he departed to interview Mr. Ellis. He found him still seated in the dining-room with Grip snuffling beside his chair. Mr. Ellis said at once, yes, the case was his. He had "scrounged" it from some stores during the War. Oh, yes, everybody knew of its existence, but he didn't think it had been taken out of the cupboard for years. If the Inspector said it seemed to have been recently dusted, he could only suppose that someone had been tidying up the bathroom. Mrs. Hulk would know. None of the drugs had ever been used, so far as he knew.

The Inspector drew his attention to the missing morphine tablets. Mr. Ellis changed colour, and seemed to grow even smaller and more crumpled than before.

"Oh," said he, uncomfortably, "yes, wait a minute. I believe I did once use a few of them — ages ago — to — to — poison a dog, you know."

"Why, what dog was that?" asked Mr. Parsons, who had attached himself firmly to the Inspector, and could not be shaken off. "I never knew you had any dog but Grip, and we've been neighbours ever since the War. Fancy you having another dog, and me not noticing! And I pride myself upon always noticing everything!"

"It wasn't my dog," said Mr. Ellis, rather unconvincingly. "Er — it was a friend's dog. A Pekinese," he added, by way of corroborative detail.

"It had canker of the ear, poor creature."

"Well, I must detain the case," said the Inspector, wrapping it up carefully, and slipping it into a handbag. "It will have to go to Headquarters to be tested for fingerprints."

"But the man was not poisoned, was he, Inspector?" said Mr. Ellis, bewildered.

"I cannot say definitely till after the autopsy," said the Inspector. "And now I should like a word with Mr. Robert Ellis."

Robert, it appeared, had gone to his bedroom, but when summoned by Wilfred, he came down in his shirt sleeves. Wilfred, remembering his embarrassed actions earlier in the evening, looked narrowly at his cuffs. They were none too clean, certainly, but the spots on them were undoubtedly ordinary black ink, which he made no effort to hide.

Robert could not help the Inspector at all. He knew nothing, and had thought Dudden had gone out to his club until the dreadful moment when the body was discovered. The sight of blood always made him feel very sick – he was sensitive that way – and he had simply *had* to bolt upstairs and lie down. He certainly looked horribly white and ill, and the Inspector mercifully released him.

"Well, now," said Inspector Rice, when Dr. Larkin had gone, reluctantly followed by Mr. Parsons, "it seems as though there might be some unpleasant characters hanging about the place. I think it will be better if I stay here tonight. No need to put Mrs. Ellis about. Any old shakedown will do for me. Then I shall be handy in case I am wanted."

It struck Wilfred that none of the family seemed to want the Inspector particularly, but nobody made any protest. They talked in dismal whispers, till the Inspector returned from making a telephone call.

"That's all right," said Rice cheerfully, "we shall be sending for the body later on. You will all feel more comfortable when that is out of the way."

"Can I go home?" asked Wilfred, rather uncertainly.

"By all means," said the Inspector. "You will let me have your address? I may want to see you again in the morning."

Wilfred gave the address, bade a subdued goodnight to Mr. and Mrs. Ellis, and stumbled drearily out. It might have been his fancy, but he felt that somebody or something was moving stealthily after him through the rain and the darkness, all the way to his lodgings.

Mr. Parsons had gone home, but not to bed. He remained at his front gate, smoking and observing, long after the street was quiet. He saw the lights in the Ellises' house go out — all except one on the first floor, which he took to be Amy's, and one in the sitting-room, where Inspector Rice kept vigil.

About one o'clock, a dismal van drove up to the little gate. Four men emerged from it with a stretcher. They went up to the house, and were let in. Presently the door opened again. A gloomy burden, swathed in black, was carried out and put in the van. The engine was started up, and the van moved away.

Mr. Parsons still stood at the gate. He thought he noticed something stirring beneath the laburnums which dripped and swung over the garden wall. At length a dark shape detached itself and sidled up to him.

"Say, Mister," said a hoarse voice in his ear.

"Eh?" said Mr. Parsons.

"Say, Mister, that was the police, wasn't it? 'As he bin an' gorn an' done it?"

"Has who done what?" said Mr. Parsons, startled.

"Mr. Robert. 'As 'e bin an' gorn an done 'isself in?"

"Why?" said Mr. Parsons. "What makes you think that? What do you know about it?"

"Me? Nuffin', Mister. I knows nuffin', s'welp me. But see 'ere. Ef yer seein' 'er — Mrs. Ellis — jest you say to 'er, it wasn't my fault. 'E never come. She'll understand. Jest you say that. *'E never come.*"

IV

IN THE ASPIDISTRA

by anthony berkeley

Detective Inspector Rice had no intention of spending that night in sleep. Other people, however, must not know that. It was therefore with some care that the Inspector walked upstairs at a quarter past one with his heaviest tread and closed his bedroom door in the most convincing way. Then he sat down on the only chair in the room and prepared for an hour's really hard thinking.

From the notes he made from time to time, it seemed that Inspector Rice did most of his thinking in questions:

Is it an outside or an inside job?

How could it possibly be an outside one?

Are the family telling all they know?

Are they shielding one of themselves?

That fellow Hope, now –

Why wouldn't Miss Ellis see me, *really*?

Who washed the bathroom floor?

Why was Mrs. Hulk cutting up beef so late?

The Inspector looked at his last entry, scratched his head, and then underlined the words in heavy black lead.

He glanced at his watch. It was nearly twenty minutes to two.

He began to make out a rough time-table of events, searching back among the pages of his notebook with a large thumb.

9:15 p.m. Dudden leaves table. Front door bangs.

9:20 p.m. Hulk seen going to back door.

9:25 p.m. Mrs. Hulk draws parlour curtains.

9:28 p.m. Family enters parlour.

9:30 p.m. Hulk seen to leave.

10:00 p.m. Hope arrives.

The Inspector's forehead was furrowed as he studied what he had written. The difficulty was obvious. Assuming that Mrs. Hulk had not practically stumbled over the body without seeing it, the time-table gave exactly three minutes for Dudden to have been stabbed and stowed away behind the screen. That was possible perhaps, but was it probable? In other words, was the time-table reliable?

The Inspector took a lick at his pencil-stub and rapidly added three more questions to his list:

Where was Dudden between 9:15 and 9:28?

Is Mrs. Ellis speaking the truth, that no one else left the dining-room alone?

Are any of them speaking the truth?

He thought for a moment and then wrote down, in despairing capitals, one last sentence:

ARE THEY ALL IN IT?

As if nothing could improve upon that, he shut his notebook with a snap and leaned back in his chair, his hands deep in his pockets. Independent witnesses — that was what he wanted: and except for that fussy little know-all next door, Parsons, there wasn't a single one.

An idea came to him. What was that about a dressmaker coming round that evening? Had she come, or hadn't she? He could not remember. But if she had she might have seen something. He must look into that tomorrow. Another idea: the probabilities all pointed to death having occurred after ten o'clock. Hope had arrived at ten o'clock. Was this significant, or not? To be so there must be some connection, and a very close connection, between the medical student and Dudden, the city man.

Out came the notebook again, and one last entry was made: Hope — Amy Ellis — Dudden. Query, connection here?

He rose to his feet, opened his bedroom door, listened without moving for at least a minute, and then crept noiselessly in the darkness down the stairs, the position of which he had carefully memorised. He was going to search, unhindered, for that knife. The time passed quickly. By a quarter past two he had searched the parlour; by half past two the kitchen. The knife remained unfound. He was about to pass into the scullery when a sound overhead brought him up stock still. Somebody was shuffling down the stairs. In three silent strides Inspector Rice had reached the kitchen light and snapped it out; in five more he was in the scullery, with the door into the kitchen half-closed; for the steps, reaching the hall, had turned unmistakably in the direction of the kitchen. The next instant the door from the hall opened, softly closed again, and the electric light sprang on. With an eye glued to the crack of the scullery door Inspector Rice watched the intruder.

It was Robert Ellis. He was in pyjamas, his feet bare, and it was plain that he was very, very frightened. In one hand he held, tightly grasped, a small bundle. He hesitated just inside the door, listening, and then hurried towards the stove. But before he could fulfil his obvious intention of thrusting the bundle down among the embers, the Inspector had hurried forward and relieved him of it.

"Thank you, Mr. Ellis," he said pleasantly. "I think perhaps I had better take charge of this." He shook it out. It was a cotton shirt, and the Inspector noticed with interest that the cuffs were stained with blood. "How do you account for this?" he asked sternly, pointing to the blood-stains.

For a moment Robert seemed unable to reply. His face was chalky, his whole body trembling so violently that his teeth chattered. Then suddenly he found his voice. "I – I got it touching *him*," he cried, half hysterically. "Before you came. When we were looking to – to see if he was dead. That's how."

"Then why did you want to burn it?"

"Because it makes me ill. Blood does. I can't stand it. Makes me feel sick. Horrible! I wouldn't wear that shirt again, not for a thousand pounds. Only thing to do was to burn it. I tell you, blood makes me ill." His voice dropped to a whimper. "What else could I do but burn it?"

"I see," said the Inspector quietly, contemplating the pitiable figure. "Well, you'd better get up to bed again, my lad. Catch a cold with those bare feet, if you're not careful."

Astonished, apparently, that he was not to be arrested, tried, sentenced and hanged on the spot, Robert gaped, then grinned feebly and scuttled away. The Inspector tenderly rolled up the shirt again. "So it was that young ninny after all, was it?" ran his thoughts. "I wouldn't have thought he'd got it in him. No wonder they were all lying their heads off. Well, it shouldn't be difficult to fix it on him now. This shirt's a real bit of luck."

If it were, it was the only bit of luck the Inspector had that night: for when, two hours later, he composed himself disgustedly on two chairs in the parlour, the door wide open, for two or three hours' very light sleep, the knife still remained elusive. Inspector Rice never doubted that the missing knife was the weapon with which the crime had been committed.

A light tapping on the window outside, just before half past seven, roused him instantly. Mr. Parsons was peering through the glass; on seeing the Inspector approach, he beckoned urgently. In the clear, early morning light he looked more mottled than ever.

Stifling a rude word, Inspector Rice threw up the window. "Now, sir, I really cannot allow you to –"

"I've got news, Inspector," broke in Mr. Parsons, in a whisper squeaky with excitement. "Positively the most important news. I knew I should find you on the scene of the crime. Instinctively! I'm like that. You remember my suggestion that this man Hulk might be a member of some gang? I was right. I'm positive I was right.

And, Inspector – Mrs. Ellis is in it, too. Listen! Last night, after –"

"One moment, sir," interrupted the patient inspector. "If you have anything to tell me, may I come over to your own house? We shan't be overheard there."

"Of course! Certainly! I shall be delighted," twittered the little man. "I'll go and open the front door at once. This very minute!" He hurried off down the path.

Outside the Inspector beckoned to the constable stationed in front of the house. "Take charge, Benson. Don't let anyone into the parlour. If I'm wanted I shall be next door."

He followed Mr. Parsons into "Swallowcliffe."

It was nearly half an hour before the Inspector had succeeded in getting the full story of Hulk's mysterious second visit, and he then asked leave to use the telephone. Mr. Parsons accorded it with enthusiasm, both for this occasion and any future one; he seemed on the point of putting his whole house and belongings at Inspector Rice's disposal. Perhaps he considered this sufficient justification for standing shamelessly by while the Inspector telephoned.

"Is that Sergeant Farrar? Inspector Rice speaking. Take this down, Farrar, please." The Inspector gave as good a description of Hulk as Mr. Parsons had been able to offer. "Yes, I want that man pulled in and held till I've seen him. Have that description circulated to all stations. Is Sergeant Hall there? No? Well, get on to him and ask him to come up here at once. That's all. No – wait a minute. Have headquarters sent the copies of those fingerprints on that black japanned case that I sent up for examination last night? Well, send them along to me as soon as they come in, please. Yes, here." Mr. Parsons almost danced with excitement. Fingerprints! This was the real thing.

The Inspector stood for a moment, thinking deeply and quite oblivious of the human question-mark that was gyrating round him. Then he took up the receiver again and gave another number. It was the police-surgeon's, but Mr. Parsons did not know that.

"Sorry to bother you so early, sir, but I'm particularly anxious to get an idea of what your report's going to be. By the way," added the Inspector cautiously, "I'm speaking from a rather public place, you understand."

There was a chuckle at the other end of the wire. "I get you. Some busybody listening, eh? Well, Inspector, I've only made a hurried autopsy, but I've sponged the wound and it seems quite straightforward. The murderer (if it was murder, and I don't think there's much doubt about that) had two attempts; the first was a shallow, slicing cut which nicked a small artery, but didn't do much damage otherwise: the second a straight stab, almost in the line of the first. That's the one that caused death. The man wouldn't have died at once, though; he must have bled to death quite slowly."

"Oh!" said the Inspector.

"As to the other thing – mind, I can't say anything definite yet, but I'm pretty sure the hint I gave you was right; the man was certainly suffering from some form of narcotic poisoning when he died. Not necessarily enough to cause death (I can't tell you that yet), but in any case quite a hefty dose."

"Ah!" said the Inspector.

"And that's really all I can tell you at present."

"Thank you, sir," said the Inspector, and rang off.

"Inspector," bubbled Mr. Parsons, "you must stay and have some breakfast now. Positively you must. I insist. My wife and I . . . the greatest pleasure."

"Well, that's very kind of you, sir," replied the Inspector, genially. "I could do with a bite of breakfast, and that's a fact." He would have to listen to some very tedious palaver, but there might be a grain or two of real information amongst the dross. And, anyhow, the Inspector wanted his breakfast.

He ate two fried eggs and made the acquaintance of Mrs. Parsons, a subdued little woman who looked at him timidly and said very little; but when he returned next door, just after nine o'clock, it was with nothing of any value (beyond the two fried eggs) to compensate for the delay.

The family, he learned from the constable, were just finishing their breakfast. Miss Ellis was still in bed, and could see no one. "Is that so?" said the Inspector.

In the drawing-room Sergeant Hall was waiting for him.

"Morning, Sergeant. Got a ticklish job for you. I want the prints of everyone in this house, and I don't want them to know you've taken them. Manage it?"

The Sergeant grinned acquiescence and went out. Inspector Rice settled himself in a chair and began to enter up in his notebook the facts he had learned this morning. There was a tap at the door and the constable came into the room; he closed the door behind him before he spoke. "That dressmaker's here, sir. Miss Pettigrew. I thought you might like to know. I heard the cook saying she came here last night, and fancied you might want to see her."

The Inspector nodded approval. "That's right. Where is she?"

The constable jerked his thumb over his shoulder and slightly opened the door. The sound trickled into the room of a thin, watery little voice, extremely refined ". . . so I thought you wouldn't want to be bothered so late, and took it away again. I don't know whether I've acted as you'd wish, Mrs. Ellis, but as soon as I saw the dreadful news in the papers, I said to myself, 'Now, a black dress is just what Mrs. Ellis will be wanting,' so I hurried round and . . ."

"The truth being," observed the Inspector, humorously, as he went out, "that as soon as she saw the dreadful news in the papers she couldn't rest till she'd got both feet in the house. They're all alike."

"That's right, sir," beamed the constable, much gratified at being the recipient of an inspectorial jest.

Firmly the Inspector detached Miss Pettigrew from Mrs. Ellis and led her into the drawing-room. She was a tall, faded woman of about forty, with tired eyes, a thin, very pink nose, and wear-

ing an indeterminate hat and grey cotton gloves.
The forthcoming interview was plainly a most unexpected development of the simple curiosity
which the Inspector had imputed to her, for, in
spite of every effort to restrain them, her hands
were trembling visibly. Inspector Rice had no
difficulty in placing her as one of that type to
whom any dealings with the police, however, innocent, are "not quite nice."

With such, tact is needed. The Inspector proceeded to apply it. With ceremony he ushered
Miss Pettigrew into a chair, in deferential tones
he apologised for the inconvenience to herself,
confidentially he hinted that Miss Pettigrew's assistance was the very thing for which the police
had been desperately longing and were prepared
almost to go down on their knees to obtain. "So
I'm sure you won't mind if I ask you just one or
two questions?" he said, unctuously.

"Not at all," replied Miss Pettigrew, in prim,
if rather quavery, tones, sitting on the extreme
edge of the most uncomfortable chair in the room.

With the same confidential air, the Inspector
proceeded to put his questions, and Miss Pettigrew gradually responded to the treatment. Her
hands ceased to tremble; her voice lost its quaver;
her long thin nose grew even a little pinker with
gratification. Certainly she would assist the
course of justice if she could. Of course she would
tell all she knew. Miss Pettigrew became almost
animated.

She had come to the back door last night, then,
at – well, it must have been just about ten minutes
past nine. Anyhow, Mrs. Hulk would know. The
family were at supper, so Mrs. Hulk had shown

her into the hall to wait. Mrs. Hulk had been —
well, perhaps, yes a little *queer*, Miss Pettigrew
had thought. She had waited in the hall about ten
minutes and then, feeling sure Mrs. Ellis would
not want to be bothered so late, had let herself
out of the front door.

The Inspector was almost rubbing his hands
with delight. This was really too good to be true.
He questioned Miss Pettigrew further, with difficulty concealing his eagerness. Yes, Miss Pettigrew had been at the far end of the hall, in the
shadow. Yes, certainly she had seen Mr. Dudden
come out of the dining-room.

"And what did he do?"

It had seemed to Miss Pettigrew, even then,
that Mr. Dudden was behaving very strangely. In
fact had she not known the household so well she
would have thought — it was a terrible thing to
say, but she really would have thought he was
drunk. He had seemed almost to *reel*, instead of
walk. And before going into the drawing-room he
had opened the front door and then simply
slammed it. Most odd!

"Yes, yes," gloated the Inspector. "He went
into the drawing-room. And then who followed
him out from the dining-room?"

Miss Pettigrew looked startled. "Who followed
him? Pardon me, I don't quite understand. Nobody followed him."

"Well, who came out next? During the next
five minutes, if you like."

"Indeed, nobody else came out of the dining-
room at all."

"What?" said the Inspector incredulously.
"Not all the time you were waiting? Oh, come,

miss, please."

Miss Pettigrew began to tremble again. "Do you – do you insinuate that I am not speaking the truth?"

The Inspector hastened to reassure her, but it was no use; though mollified, Miss Pettigrew could not say, even to oblige the Inspector, that anyone else had followed Mr. Dudden from the dining-room for the simple reason that nobody had.

"Not even Robert Ellis?" blurted out the Inspector at last.

"Certainly not," replied Miss Pettigrew, in tones of high offence at this fresh insinuation.

The Inspector had to let her go. He did so ruefully. From being too good to be true, Miss Pettigrew had become too bad. This seemed almost to let Robert Ellis out altogether. But did it, though? The Inspector walked round behind the screen. That window, now. . . .

A tap at the door interrupted his thoughts. Sergeant Hall came into the room. He wore an air of triumph. "Quite a lot of news come through in a rush, sir. First, I've got all those prints for you."

"Ah!" said the Inspector. He did not waste time asking how this difficult task had been effected; that was taken for granted.

"And a photograph of those prints on the japanned medicine case has come through from headquarters. They're the girl's all right – Amy Ellis. Not a shadow of doubt."

"Ah!" said the Inspector again. The news did not seem to surprise him very much. "Anything else?"

"Yes, they've got Hulk. Down at Wapping. They're holding him for you, but they've taken his story themselves, to save time. This is what he says." Sergeant Hall gave the story concisely. Hulk had admitted to having accepted money from Mrs. Ellis to lie in wait for Dudden the previous evening, knock him out, and get possession of his pocket-book. He did not know why the pocket-book was wanted. Not for the money in it, he was sure; he had gathered that it contained some paper or other which Mrs. Ellis was desperately anxious to obtain.

"Phew!" whistled the Inspector. "What's all this about? I've been through that pocket-book myself. There's no paper of *that* sort in it."

"It all hangs together, sir," Sergeant Hall countered triumphantly. "Merriman telephoned through immediately afterwards." Detective Constable Merriman had been detailed to go down to Dudden's office in the City first thing that morning and make a preliminary examination of his possessions there. "I didn't interrupt you because he's on his way here now. He says he found nothing of interest, papers all in order and all that, *except* – in an envelope in Dudden's office safe there's a cheque for a hundred and fifty pounds marked 'Signature Differs' and a signed confession by Robert Ellis that the cheque's a forgery executed by himself." Sergeant Hall's broad smile indicated that in his opinion the case was as good as ended.

The Inspector seemed to agree. "Right! That about clinches it, weapon or no weapon. We'll have Master Robert Ellis on the mat, I think, Sergeant. Bring him along, and then stand by."

As the Sergeant went out, Inspector Rice called the constable in from the hall. "Telephone to Sergeant Farrar to get a warrant made out, Benson," he said in a low voice. "Name, Robert Ellis; charge, murder. Not from here. Better go next door."

The constable nodded and disappeared. A moment later Sergeant Hall came into view, half-dragging and half-driving the pimply youth through the doorway.

Inspector Rice confronted his victim from the hearthrug. "Now then, Ellis, you'd better tell us all about it," he said sternly. "It'll be better for you in the end. Come along."

"I don't know what you mean," Robert almost shrieked. "I haven't anything to tell. Damn you, let me go upstairs!"

"Don't you take that tone, my lad. Nothing to tell, eh? That's pretty good. What about that cheque of Dudden's you forged? What about that confession you wrote out? Come along, now – what have you done with that knife?"

The Inspector paused. He had purposely adopted a bullying tone as the best means of countering the youth's incipient hysteria. But there was no need to continue it. The news of the discovery of the forged cheque seemed to have knocked out what little anaemic stuffing there had been in Robert. He had tumbled into the nearest chair and sat there, twitching and shivering, his pimply forehead glistening in panic. To the Inspector's practised eye he was obviously on the point of confession. "I – I – I," he mouthed.

"There is no need for you to bully my son, Inspector," said a quiet but rather shaky voice from the door.

The Inspector wheeled round angrily. "Madam, I really must ask you to remain outside. I said that —"

"And *I* said there was no need for you to bully my son," interposed Mrs. Ellis calmly. "I'm quite ready to tell you the truth. *I* killed Mr. Dudden."

His anger forgotten, the Inspector stared at her in astonishment. The confession had taken him completely by surprise. And yet it was reasonable enough. That story of Hulk's . . .

He became aware of Constable Benson beckoning eagerly from the doorway, and went out mechanically. Constable Benson seemed extremely pleased with himself. With pride he displayed to the Inspector's gaze, holding it carefully by the edges, a bloodstained surgical knife. "Fancy this is what you've been looking for, isn't it, sir? Thought I might as well have a look round next door when I'd done telephoning, and I found this — well, it was hid away in Mr. Parsons' aspidistra, sir."

V

by e. c. bentley

Inspector Rice whistled gently and expres-
sively, as he drew out his handkerchief and mo-
tioned to the constable to lay the knife upon it.
Carrying the blood-stained instrument thus on
his open right hand he turned to re-enter the
drawing-room. "You want me?" inquired Sergeant Hall, who had observed this unexpected
development with a gleam in his hard blue eye.
"Of course," the Inspector said. "Things are beginning to happen quite rapidly, Sergeant, You –"
to the gratified Constable Benson – "stand by
this door."

Carrying the knife ostentatiously displayed,
the Inspector entered the room, followed by his
satellite, and walked to the table where the open
case of instruments lay. He was not disappointed
of his effect. Mrs. Ellis shrieked and covered her
face with her hands; her son, with a choking gasp,
sprang from his chair, and then collapsed into it
again shuddering violently.

"It's the missing knife right enough," the Inspector observed as he compared it with those in the case. He walked with the Sergeant to the window, where with backs turned to the mother and son they spoke in low tones. "You've got your fingerprint doings here?" the Inspector asked. "In the next room," was the answer. "That's right; and you've got the prints of the household. Take this weapon and report as soon as you've finished testing." The Sergeant received his charge with delicate fingers. "One or two pretty good impressions visible to start with," he murmured. "Done with bloody fingers, those are. And –" he held the knife to the light at an angle – "there are others, I can see; they should be easily brought out."

At a slight sound from behind them Inspector Rice whipped round. "You stay here, my lad," he barked sharply, "and keep away from those knives" – as the wretched Robert, taking his hand from the door-handle, turned unsteadily in the direction of the open case. As he fell into his chair again, his mother went to him and laid a hand on his shoulder. "You have no right to speak to my son like that," she cried violently. "He has done nothing wrong."

"He looks like it," the Inspector remarked harshly. "All right, Sergeant, go to it. Now, Madam" – as his subordinate went out – "will you repeat to me the very surprising statement you made a few minutes ago?"

"I told you that I killed him," Mrs. Ellis said, clasping her trembling hands together. "I killed him. And I won't say another word. You can arrest me now."

The Inspector stroked his chin. This was not turning out so easily. Had she, after all, done it? As a confession, her statement was suspicious to a degree. He knew already — assuming Hulk's story to be true — that for her son's sake the old lady was prepared to go to pretty desperate lengths. This was, he thought, a case in which a little low cunning would be in order.

"But surely," he said slowly, "you might at least tell me —"

Mrs. Ellis shook her head obstinately. "Not another word. I won't be trapped."

Inspector Rice's expression brightened. Here was a person demanding to be sent to the scaffold, and refusing to be trapped. Such simplicity, he thought, was all too rare. "But," he said, "your confession, Mrs. Ellis, is really very difficult to believe."

"I killed him," she repeated dully.

"You really mean to tell me" — here the Inspector made use of a wagging forefinger — "that you turned on this man — a man with whom you had been on a friendly footing for years — that you took a knife and stabbed him to the heart?"

"Yes, I do say so," she replied sharply. "And I'll say nothing more."

The Inspector shook his head. "You need say nothing more, ma'am," he observed more gently. "You have just said all that is necessary. And now" — he turned swiftly upon Robert Ellis — "what about your having done nothing wrong? You agree with your mother about that, do you?"

For the first time since the Inspector had seen him the young man had pulled himself together. He stood up now, white and calm. "You sneering swine," he said, "you know I'm guilty, I believe. Anyhow, you needn't think I was going to let my mother take my place, even if you had believed her. I am through. I murdered Dudden, I never meant to do it, but I did it."

Mrs. Ellis clutched the Inspector's arm. "It's a falsehood," she gasped. "You can't believe him. He's saying it to shield me. I tell you it was I —"

"It isn't any use, mother," the young man said wearily. "I'm rotten, I know, but there are some things I can't do. I am going to tell the whole thing; I've made up my mind, and I feel better now than I've felt any time since it happened. We all had our reasons for hating Dudden. We all knew he was pestering Amy to marry him, though she was as good as engaged to Wilfred Hope. The very night when it happened, Father was going to tell him he must go; but Dudden had lent him money, and was certain to be nasty about it, the bullying brute. As for me, you've found out what I had done, it seems."

Inspector Rice produced his notebook. "If you wish to make a confession," he said formally, "I am ready to take down in shorthand what you say, and to make a copy for you to read through and sign."

It was a wretched story that the young man told, while his mother sat weeping hopelessly beside him. He had been betting – he had had losses far more heavy than he could meet; he was being pressed mercilessly for payment, was sure of losing his position if the facts became known. He knew that Dudden kept a cheque-book in his room, and the crazy scheme of forgery came into

his mind. He had stolen a cheque and forged
Dudden's name; at the bank the fraud had been
detected at once, payment had been refused and
the cheque retained.

When Dudden received the forged cheque
from his bankers he had jumped immediately to
a right conclusion as to the identity of the forger.
Robert had intended, if his plan failed, to deny
everything to the last and to count on Dudden's
unwillingness to proceed to extremes against the
brother of the girl whom he desired to marry. But
he was now to discover that the man was capable
of baseness greater than his own. Dudden had
taxed him with the crime, and had soon bullied
and threatened the spineless youth into a complete surrender. Dudden had then laid down his
terms. No more would be said about the forgery
if Robert would hand to Dudden his written
confession, and would use his influence with
Amy in favour of Dudden's proposal of marriage.
How could he possibly influence his sister's decision in such a matter? Dudden, asked this question, had laughed brutally and said that that was
Robert's business; that it ought not to take him
long to think of a way to persuade his sister. Anyhow, there the proposition was. On the day of
Dudden's marriage to Amy, the confession and
the cheque would be returned to Robert; if Amy's
consent was not forthcoming within a fortnight,
both documents would be handed to the police.

Robert, cornered and helpless, had at last
agreed to this. Then, seeing, as Dudden had so
clearly seen, that Amy would be moved by nothing short of knowing the whole disgraceful story,
he had told her everything. What followed was

to have been foreseen. Amy, again and again, had pleaded desperately with Dudden to have mercy on her brother and herself; he had been quite unmoved, and had demanded her final decision by a certain evening — the evening of the murder. What Amy had intended then to say or to do, Robert did not know. She had steadfastly refused to tell him what was in her mind.

When, at dinner that evening, Dudden had left the company early, saying that he was going out, the half-frantic Robert had risen also on an impulse, and followed him from the room. He had seen Dudden open and close the front door, and then enter the drawing-room; he had guessed that Amy was shortly to join Dudden for the final interview before her parents left the table. Robert, hardly knowing what he did, had hastily taken a knife from Wilfred's case where it lay on the hall table; some vague idea of threatening Dudden was in his disordered thoughts as he followed his torturer into the empty room.

What Robert now told the Inspector caused that officer to glance up from his stenography with a look of the liveliest interest. Dudden, when confronted by the young man in the drawing-room and assailed with wild words, had acted very strangely. Instead of taking at once to his usual bullying tone, he had stood silent, leaning on a chair with eyes half-closed, and apparently paying not the slightest attention to Robert's words, or even to his presence. Robert, taking this for a show of contemptuous indifference, had then lost all control of his emotions. He had leaped at the man, aiming a blow at his throat; and at that moment Dudden had staggered, so that the knife struck him on the side of the neck. It had not, Robert felt, been a deep wound; but there had been a spurting of blood over his hands, and Dudden had fallen first on his knees, and then at full length, on the spot where the body was afterwards found.

"Wait a minute," put in the Inspector. "There was a strong spurt of blood, was there? Do you happen to know – I have a reason for asking – whether Mr. Dudden was a man who bled very easily?"

Robert looked puzzled. "I – I do not know. I think . . . No, I do not know."

"All right; never mind. Go on."

Robert, appalled at what he had done, had then rushed from the room and hurried at once to the bathroom to wash the blood from his hands, on a desperate impulse of concealment. He had found then, to his further dismay, that there were bloodstains on the cuffs of his shirt; but he dared not take the time to change the garment. He had hastened downstairs again and taken his seat in the drawing-room until his parents and his sister came and joined him there.

It was at this point in Robert's narrative that Inspector Rice looked up to put a question. "Then you put up the screen in front of the body," he said, "before the others came into the room."

The young man shook his head. "I never touched the screen at all," he declared. "It was there all the time. Dudden was behind it, leaning on a chair, when I went up to him. There was plenty of space behind the screen."

"We'll see just how it was," the Inspector said; and he lifted the screen from the place where it now rested against the wall. Assisted now by Robert, he set it up as it had been when he was first called to the scene of the crime; and in this Inspector Rice had a certain purpose. For he had been struck by a curious discrepancy in the account that the young man had given of what took place. The officer's professional experience assured him that what he had been hearing was the truth; and yet —

"You have said everything that happened when the man was killed?" he inquired. "It will be best to get it absolutely right, you know."

Robert protested that he had omitted nothing. He had no objection to showing exactly how the thing had happened. The Inspector standing as the murdered man had stood, Robert demonstrated precisely how and where he had struck the blow. It was evident to Inspector Rice that there was something very queer about the whole affair as it was now presented; queer in more than one respect.

And yet the confessed murderer was telling what he had done exactly as it had happened. Rice was convinced of that. The young man's whole demeanour showed it; from a cringing poltroon he had changed to a man — not a particularly admirable sort of man, but at least a man with the kind of moral strength which comes of making a clean breast of it and facing the music. The Inspector had seen that phenomenon often enough to be able to recognise it infallibly. It could not be acted; and even if it could, Robert Ellis emphatically was not the sort who could act it.

But if it simply was not possible to accept Robert's story of the affair as accounting for all the very puzzling and sinister facts known to him, in what direction was he to look for light?

The Inspector told himself reproachfully that there was one very obvious direction that he had been overlooking. It could not be doubted that Robert had been telling the truth. But what about the whole truth? If any other persons had any hand in the affair, it was by no means out of the question that Robert Ellis knew something about it. And Inspector Rice had to know. As things stood, he was far – very far – from having a clean case.

He decided to draw a bow at a venture.

"What you have told me, then," he said, "is the full extent of your confession to the murder of Paul Dudden? I have got down everything as it happened?

Robert showed a little uneasiness at the pointed questioning. "Yes," he said, "that's right."

"Quite sure?" And at this pressing the young man's uncertain self-control failed utterly. "Sure – yes," he stammered. "There – there was nobody else."

"But I didn't suggest, you know, that there was anybody else," the Inspector pointed out. There was a pause, Robert glaring mutely at his interrogator, and evidently resolved to say no more. Inspector Rice at length said in his most persuasive tone, "You must understand that there is other evidence in my hands than your own – a great deal of other evidence, I may say; and that it tends to incriminate other members of this household." And as Robert remained silent, the Inspector added slowly, "Come, I think I understand, and I don't say that it doesn't do you credit. But if she was —"

"What I have told you is God's truth," Robert broke out fiercely. "I tell you that when I did it she — nobody else was here."

This was quite enough for Inspector Rice. Opening the door, he signed to the waiting constable without. "Let Miss Ellis know," he said, "that I wish to see her, and that it is important that no more time should be lost."

Mrs. Ellis, who still sat weeping quietly in the background, had heard all this with signs of renewed agitation. "He can't bring Amy into it," she wailed. "He can't have anything against Amy. Oh dear, isn't it enough to have one of them taken from me?"

Her lamentations ceased suddenly as her daughter appeared with unexpected promptitude in the doorway. Amy had evidently overcome the emotions which were understood to have prostrated her so completely. She was pale and worn, but she had an air of composure and even of determination, and without so much as a glance at Inspector Rice she turned a look of inquiry on her brother.

"It's all over," Robert said in answer to her unspoken question. "I've told him the whole thing."

The girl turned to Inspector Rice. "That is impossible," she said in a hard voice. "He cannot have told you everything, for he doesn't know everything. But if he has told all about Dudden and myself, as I suppose he has — and anyhow you would have to know it — then I have something more to say."

The Inspector had turned to her with a look of gratified expectation that he did not try to disguise. But before he could reply to her, Sergeant Hall showed himself at the door, and in response to a nod from the Inspector walked with him to the window, where again they conferred in undertones.

"His prints are on the knife?" Rice asked, with a motion of his head towards Robert.

"Plain as can be. But," added the Sergeant, "it's a queer thing about the others – the bloody ones, that is. You see they are all on the top of his wherever they come together. It's evident what that means."

"Yes, of course, it is," the Inspector answered tartly. "I wasn't born yesterday. But do you know whose they are – the second lot?"

Sergeant Hall smiled in appreciation of the effect that he was now to make. "They're the old woman's," he whispered.

"What?" Rice was really startled. "Great Scott! Then can she have been telling the truth after all?"

"I don't know what she's been telling you," his subordinate replied with relish. "I didn't know you had been putting her through it. But they're Mrs. Hulk's fingerprints all right."

VI

MR. PARSONS ON THE CASE

by father ronald knox

There is kindliness even in the most warped natures; and Mr. Parsons, the "mottled man from next door," willingly asked Wilfred Hope to stay the night with him and be near the scene of action, after that harassing evening when he had seen his future brother-in-law, Robert Ellis, detained by the police for further enquiry; while his fiancée Amy and her parents continued to enjoy the shelter of their own roof only under supervision, and very obvious supervision, from the police. Mr. Parsons even brought up some whisky after dinner for Wilfred's sake, and sat there watching him with evident kindness over the rim of his barley-water.

"I feel so hopeless," Wilfred was saying. "I now know, from themselves, all the movements of the Ellises during yesterday evening and I know that none of them dealt Dudden his *coup de grâce*. That remains a mystery; and who knows what case the police are hatching up, to cover their own ignorance?"

Mr. Parsons' behaviour was peculiar. He went to the dining-room sideboard, and opened, most unexpectedly, a sliding panel in the wall. "I am proud of this," he said. "Put it in myself. Goes into the pantry, you see. The little window where the ham comes peeping in at morn. And I sometimes call it my confessional; you see, I can go into the pantry, and listen to every word that is being said in here. I did that this afternoon, you know, when Inspector Rice borrowed this room and had his interview with the real criminal."

"The real criminal? Then you know . . . ? Oh, for God's sake tell me the name; don't dance around like that."

"Come, come, Mr. Hope; let us have confidences on both sides. You know the story from the other side, the Ellises' side. Tell me that first, and I promise you you shall have my share."

"Very well, you shall have it. But you shall have it in a nutshell form, if you won't tell me your side first. There were three plots on foot that night; they all enter into the story, though none was murderous. Dudden had insisted that Amy should have an interview with me, and break off our engagement; he himself was to be listening behind the screen. When he left the dinner-table, he slammed the front door, and crept in there to hide himself behind the screen, ready for the interview. Mrs. Ellis, thinking that he really meant to leave the house, had arranged to have him shadowed by that man Hulk, knocked out with a life-preserver and robbed of certain documents."

"What documents?" put in Mr. Parsons sharply.

"A cheque, if you must know, forged in Dudden's name by Robert; and Robert's signed confession that he had forged it. This, of course, never came off; Hulk came round to get his final directions and his pay, but as Dudden never left the house, he waited for him in vain."

"And the third plot?"

"That was Amy's. I had suspected something of the sort, from the way she used to ask me, this last week or so, about the effects of narcotics. I am a medical student, you see. Well, she got hold of some morphine, and managed to put it into the beer Dudden drank at supper. Her idea was that he would go off under its influence while he waited behind the screen, and she would get the documents out of his pocket. Actually, as we now know, they were in Dudden's office."

Mr. Parsons suddenly went off into a little explosion of laughter. "I say," he cried, "that's good. It wasn't Dudden's cheque at all; it was a dud'un. See what I mean?"

"For the Lord's sake shut up, and let me get on. When he left the table, Robert followed him, on an impulse; he wanted to make one last appeal, I suppose. As he passed through the hall, he saw my case of knives, and took one out; for self-defence, he says, Dudden, when he found him in the drawing-room, was already feeling dazed with the drug, and seemed to take no notice of him. This infuriated him, and he struck at his neck with the knife. Dudden fell like a log; there was not much blood at the time, but Robert, knowing nothing about the morphine, thought he had done his man in. He found blood on his hand and cuffs, and rushed upstairs to wash. He did not reckon on Mrs. Hulk going to pull the curtains; which she did a few minutes later – about twenty-five past nine – and found a corpse, so she says, behind the screen."

"Didn't Robert expect that the rest of the family would go into the drawing-room?"

"Why, no; Amy had arranged that they should go on sitting in the dining-room till after I came; she said she wanted particularly to see me alone in the drawing-room. They were accustomed to that; though Mr. Ellis didn't like it, because his patience-table is in the drawing-room. No, it was Mrs. Hulk who found the body; and she ran upstairs to see what Robert was doing. They came down together, and looked for the papers, which weren't there. Then Mrs. Hulk took the knife, and went off to the kitchen; at that moment, they heard the rest of the family leaving the dining-room after all, and coming into the drawing-room. Robert hadn't the courage to confess what he had done. He sat down and listened to the reading, hoping that nothing would be found before they all went to bed; he thought he would bury the body in the garden, poor fool, later on."

"And that was how you found them? Robert knowing that Dudden lay dead behind the screen; Miss Amy thinking that Dudden lay drugged behind the screen; Mrs. Ellis hoping that Dudden lay clubbed on the road; altogether one of these pleasant evenings round the fireside. But something, you say, is left unexplained?"

"Everything is left unexplained. Robert is quite certain he only struck one blow, and a light one. But there was a second blow, a deep stab, which caused death. I can't believe Mrs. Hulk did it; she swears she thought the man was dead when she found him. In those five minutes, or thereabouts, say between twenty past and twenty five past, somebody must have come in and dealt the second blow. What are we to make of that? And how is Robert's counsel to explain that? You say you know who is the real criminal; I've told you everything; now it's your turn."

"Singular, very singular. And yet it all seems to fit. As I say, I was taking the liberty of listening behind the panel, at about five this afternoon. And I heard that little dressmaker – Pettigrew, isn't it, her name? – confessing to Inspector Rice that she found the corpse in the drawing-room just after twenty past, and stuck the knife in again hard to make sure that it was a corpse."

"The – the dressmaker, did you say? But why on earth should she? How did she come there? She must be mad."

"I don't think so. You see, Rice had been investigating Dudden's past life, and found that he had a wife living, whom he had deserted; her maiden name was Pettigrew. Then, looking through Mrs. Ellis's bills, he found that Miss Pettigrew had supplied her with goods ridiculously below cost price; she was making an excuse, evidently, to have the *entrée* into the house where her faithless husband lived. She was waiting in the hall for Dudden to pass through; she had just learned that he wanted to marry Miss Amy. She went in to have it out with him; found him, apparently, a corpse, and made a safe job of it. She wore gloves; she was very genteel. Then she opened the front door and slipped out. That was just before twenty-five past, while I was out posting my letters; otherwise I should have seen her."

"Then . . . then, it's all right? The murder charge will be brought against her, poor little thing? And Robert, at the worst, can only be convicted of a murderous attack. Thank God for that, anyhow!"

"Yes," said Mr. Parsons, "I think that is what will happen. Of course, if I explained my theory to the police, it might make them think twice; but I'm not one to make trouble."

"Your theory? What do you mean?"

"Don't you see that both the confessions are untrue? That it was really Miss Pettigrew who went in first, and inflicted a slight cut on Dudden's neck; Robert who went in afterwards and polished him off?"

"But this is monstrous! Why on earth should they both lie like that?"

"Robert knows that the second blow was the fatal one, therefore he pretends that he dealt the first. Miss Pettigrew thinks that the first blow was fatal; therefore she pretends that she dealt the second. If she was in the hall, why did not Robert see her there? If she was in the hall, why did she not admit that she had seen Robert passing through? Answer, she was no longer in the hall when Robert went through; she had escaped after inflicting a light wound on her unworthy husband. I fancy that Robert and Mrs. Hulk have put up a false story about the time, and that the rest of the family have been persuaded into backing them up. I fancy Robert's second thrust was given a few minutes before your arrival, and that explains why the bleeding went on so long. You yourself were surprised, you told me, at the way the corpse bled."

"I know, but I've been looking it up since. Taylor says if you don't manage to sever any of the important vessels, only branches of them, you can bleed to death as slowly as you like. He gives a case of seven hours. So there's nothing in that, really."

"Well, let us pass that. I still say that if Miss Pettigrew was in the hall when Robert came through, they would have seen one another, and it would have come out in the evidence. There was no reason why either should screen the other. Miss Pettigrew was let into the hall at ten minutes past nine, Mrs. Hulk says. When Robert left the dining-room she was no longer there. Therefore, I say, she had already stabbed Dudden, lightly, as it proved, and gone away. Robert must have inflicted the second blow, not earlier than 9:25."

"You don't convince me. Robert might have deceived the Inspector; I do not think he could have deceived his own family. And it was from Mrs. Ellis I had the whole story."

"Why, yes; I suppose that satisfies *you*. But, you see, I have been asking myself this long time past whether the whole of the family was not "in it" to some extent. Did Robert really leave them in the dark? Or did they know, even when you came into the room, what was behind the screen?"

"Excuse me," said Wilfred, rather stiffly. "You forget that I know these people, and trust them absolutely."

"Of course, of course." Mr. Parsons waved a deprecating hand. "But I was thinking what a British jury would make of it. Come, man, you yourself noticed, when you came into the room, a *general* atmosphere of nervousness. Doesn't it look as if they were all in the secret already? And had sat down to their reading at the last moment, *to make you think* they were at their ease?"

"I did think of that – I took the book Mrs. Ellis was reading and read it out to myself from the beginning of the chapter to the point they had reached when I came in; it took exactly twenty-five minutes. Was that coincidence?"

"But the Patience. Mr. Ellis was not really playing, you told me so yourself. He was only turning over the cards."

"Which shows that he was *not* nervous. A nervous man *plays* the game, to calm his nerves. Mr. Ellis was giving a signal to his wife. When he showed a particular card, she was to stop reading, and they would leave Amy and me alone together. It was the three of clubs: *Two's company*, you see, *three's none* – that was the idea."

"Well, let us absolve the family. But I still have the feeling – excuse me – that Master Robert has *not* made a clean breast of it to anyone. I am sure it was he who dealt the fatal stab."

"Yes, Mr. Parsons, but there is one thing you have overlooked. You saw the bathroom light go on, when Robert rushed upstairs to wash his hands. It was after that you went out to post your letter. And it was while you were posting the letter, and could not see the front door, that Miss Pettigrew escaped."

"You have me there. Yes, you have me. By the way, what part did Mrs. Hulk play in all this?"

"She found the knife by the corpse, and took it away wrapped in a piece of paper. That was the paper on which, afterwards, she sliced the beef, to hide the bloodstains. How she got rid of the knife I never discovered."

"That was when I came in. When the police arrived, she came round to my window, which was open, crying *'Oh, Gawd! Murder!'* I rushed out to the front door, and while I did so she slipped the knife into *my* aspidistra. She is a clever woman."

"She is. It was she who put ink on Robert's clean shirt, all over the cuffs, for fear I might have seen the bloodstains on the one he was wearing. By the way, Mr. Parsons, at one moment I suspected *you*."

"Because of the aspidistra? I think I could make good my alibi. I saw the bathroom light go up; how, if I was not at my study window? I went out to post a letter, but I was back in my room a few minutes later, and saw Hulk go. Had I time, during those twelve minutes, to force my way into the house? It was a wet and windy night, remember, and the window, naturally, was shut."

So the two amateurs pieced it out together. They could not know everything. They could not know that Miss Pettigrew, instead of waiting in the hall all the time, went into the pantry to sneak biscuits, and so never saw Robert pass. That only came out at the inquest; and was used by the court, most unscrupulously, as evidence that Miss Pettigrew was, at the moment of the murder, insane.

APPENDIX I

A Chance for Amateur Detectives

The Listener, June 25, 1930

We publish herewith details of the competition set by Mr. Milward Kennedy (author of the well-know detective novel *The Corpse on the Mat*) in connection with our serial thriller "Behind the Screen." Though these questions are appearing after the second instalment, *answers should not be sent in until after the fifth instalment has been broadcast*, and must reach the Editor of THE LISTENER by first post on Saturday, July 19. Envelopes should be marked "Behind the Screen" on the top left-hand corner.

Mr. Kennedy writes: "My main difficulty consists in my anxiety on the one hand not to spoil the listeners' amusement by asking questions which anticipate 'revelations' to be made in the third, fourth and fifth instalments; and on the other not to ask questions which may be interesting before, say, the third instalment but which are categorically answered by the story before the final instalment is reached.

"There is also, of course, the general difficulty of "playing fair." I have set my questions without having any knowledge myself of the final instalment; but I have seen synopses of the first four, and I think that most of my questions can be answered, with some confidence, after the fourth – and listeners will be able to hear the fifth instalment before they make their final decisions. I do not deny that the element of conjecture as well as deduction may enter in, but that, I think, is part of the fun; and if competitors disagree – well, I can only express my regret!

"One final word: I make bold to disagree with THE LISTENER when it lays down a maxim that sufficient clues should be supplied *by the middle of the story* to enable the solution to be guessed. My view is less mathematical; the essential thing in a 'fair' detective story seems to me to be *at some point before the 'official solution' is given in the story* to place the reader in possession of all the relevant facts. In the case of the present competition, solutions obviously must be sent in at one of five points; and the point chosen is the latest possible one – that is, before the last instalment, in which the 'official solution' will be made known."

THE QUESTIONS

A.   What solution will be reached at the end of the story as to:

1.   Whether Paul Dudden's death was Murder, Suicide or Accident?

2. Whether a narcotic was administered to Paul Dudden without his knowledge before his death? If so, when was it administered? With what motive?

3. By whom were the wounds in Dudden's neck inflicted?
    With what weapon or weapons?
    When?
    Where?
    With what motive?

4. Who removed the weapon (or weapons) with which the wound were caused? And when?

B. What persons knew, when Wilfred Hope entered the drawing-room on the night of the discovery, that Dudden's dead body lay behind the screen?

C. (i) If your reply to question A(1) is either "Suicide" or "Accident," then, in not more than 200 words, outline how, in your opinion, a charge of murder could be brought against one or more persons, and what persons.
    (ii) If your reply to question A(1) is "Murder," then state against what person or persons the police will bring a charge and, in not more than 200 words, outline the strongest arguments available for the defence.

It will be seen that questions C(i) and C(ii) are alternative; brevity and clarity should be features of the replies in either case.

Report on the Competition
The Listener, July 30, 1930

May I begin by congratulating the competitors on their efforts? I judge that they enjoyed the story as much as I did, and I also enjoyed reading their "solutions." They included at all events two very youthful yet observant essayists in Geoffrey N. Wills and Alfred Garner; and I fancy that these were not the only two. I am afraid that some competitors did not read my questions very carefully; to others perhaps I owe an apology, if the intention of my third main question (Cii, in particular) was not clear.

The questions grouped together as A dealt with the "facts" which would be established by the official solution. Competitors were not asked whether they thought that Paul Dudden had been murdered, but whether the official solution would declare he had been.

Question B was in the nature of a test of reasoning. Assuming that a candidate answered all the "questions of fact" correctly, he or she should have been able to answer B correctly, whether or not the final instalment specifically gave the answer. I judged that by the end of the story all these questions must have been categorically answered; and I imagined that several of them would have been answered before the last instalment was reached. Some of them I only put in to avoid spoiling the early instalments; and because of the further questions consequent upon them.

Question C was intended to give competitors an opportunity to put forward an alternative theory to the one which they judged would be the "official" one, and so to show their grasp of the details revealed by successive instalments. In A, I avoided putting the question, "If Dudden was murdered, who murdered him?" I left that to C. I intended that competitors who had replied "Murder" to A 1, should say in reply to C: "The police will charge Miss Pettigrew; but in her defence it can be argued . . ." To my surprise a number of competitors, having, by their replies to A as a whole, made it clear that the official solution would show that Robert Ellis, let us say, dealt the fatal blow, went on to guess that the police would charge Mrs. Hulk with the murder.

Off on a False Scent

This has added to my difficulty in judging the replies. However, it was clear to me that an incorrect answer to A 1 ruled out a competitor; inevitably it involved incorrect answers to other parts of A and to B, and I think it would be generally agreed that the most important thing was to spot that it was a case of murder, and to guess by whom the murder was committed. Not very many gave "suicide," but a surprising number (about 60) gave "accident." Can they have been influenced by the fact that Father Knox has been known in his books to come to that conclusion? I think that these competitors ought to have been warned by the difficulty which they encountered in explaining how the "accident" happened: the scalpel, apparently, had either to "stick" in the first, slicing wound and then, as Dudden fell, contrive to make the deeper wound, or else it had to lodge itself in a convenient (or, if you like, inconvenient) position on the floor. The most ingenious solutions were, I think, (a) that Grip the bulldog did the deed (this seemed to presuppose that he had One Long Tooth), and (b) that Dudden must have been a haemophiliac. One of the two authors of this latter suggestion very properly and gleefully anticipated a superb wrangle amongst expert witnesses at the trial! Perhaps I should add that many of the "no murder" group produced strong cases against various characters: one went so far as to claim an "unanswerable case" against Robert Ellis!

I think that A 1 was an easy question to answer; and so was A 2 – by the way, several competitors here (and in other questions) did themselves no good by answering more than they were asked. A 3 became rather a decisive question; and here again competitors perhaps went rather out of their way to meet trouble by deciding that one of the stabs was "fatal." Apart from this, however, my opinion is that readers (or listeners) ought to have spotted the "weak links": for example, the importance of Miss Pettigrew's presence in the hall and the fact that she did not see Robert cross it – or say that she had done so; the fact that Mr. Parsons got to know about the murder so soon; the fact that no one saw Miss Pettigrew leave the house; and (for those who selected Mr. Parsons as the villain of the piece) the fairly safe conclusion that someone would surely have commented upon the window being open on such a night, had it been found so. And there were other similar points. I should say that the competitors as a whole spotted them all (for example, Miss Greet guessed how the scalpel found its way to Mr. Parsons' aspidistra): but few, if any, spotted all of them.

Three competitors came out of A 1, 2, and 3 with flying colours (one of them, by the way, sent in two solutions). A fourth fell but little short – as a result of "volunteering" a wrong answer to an unasked question. Three more were close behind, having inverted the order of events. By deciding that Miss Pettigrew did her stabbing before Robert, they went astray as to the weapon used by her, and its method of disposal; and one of the three leaders stumbled over the same questions. I might remark that the majority of those who guessed "murder," guessed that the first and slighter wound was caused by Robert, the second by Mrs. Hulk.

None of the seven "leaders" answered B correctly. The nearest reply (of Miss E. M. Jones) was that Robert, Mrs. Hulk and Miss Pettigrew "knew" that Dudden's dead body lay behind the screen when Hope entered the room. I would stretch a point and accept Mrs. Hulk as "knowing" this; but Wilfred did not enter the room till nearly forty minutes after Miss Pettigrew had left the house – she could hardly "know" that the body was still there. Three who had fallen behind on A (Miss Overton, Mr. Abrams and Mr. Munro) made up some lost ground. The replies of Mr. Jackson Wilkes and of Mr. Payne were not only wrong (according to the "official solution"), but were in themselves illogical.

There was a collapse at Question C. Quite apart from the preference for selecting as the "person against whom the police will bring a charge" some other person than the one whom the official solution would adjudge to have delivered the "fatal" blow, many competitors apparently thought that the best defence was an appeal to sentiment. Only Mr. J. Wilkes, Mr. Munro and Mr. Abrams, of the competitors mentioned above, put forward any other defence. Of these three, Mr. Abrams (who moreover said that the charge would be against Miss Pettigrew) gave by far the best reply, even though some of his arguments were unsound because he had not answered the earlier questions correctly. Surely the obvious line of defence would consist in arguing that the evidence pointed at least as strongly to another culprit – or to other culprits? Personally I think that that would be so even after the sixth instalment. Robert, after all, confessed to an assault, and talked of "blood spurting out," and the screen was splashed, was it not? He had believed that Dudden was dead – suppose he had been right? Then again, is not Mrs. Hulk's evidence decidedly suspect? Nor are these the only lines to be followed: I will cite only one other point which still is puzzling me – "Why did Mrs. Ellis scream when she saw a little moist patch on the floor by the screen?" Because it was blood? Come now: an old lady reading aloud in a gas-lit room looks up and sees a wet mark and knows at once that it is blood? The theory may "grip" the imagination but . . . The winner even guessed that Miss Pettigrew was Dudden's deserted wife; yet she did not argue that murder is not the simplest way of preventing bigamy.

The Winners

One last word: of some 170 answers only very few closely associated Miss Pettigrew with the murder; it seems only fair, as I have said, to make this a decisive test. After careful consideration I think that the first prize of *Ten Guineas* goes to Miss E. M. Jones (Harborne, Birmingham) in view of the excellence of her answers to A and B; the second, of *Five Guineas*, to Mr. J. T. Abrams (Grimsby), whose reply to C offset some of his earlier errors; and that the third prize of *Two Guineas* should be divided between Mr. D. Jackson Wilkes (Farnham, Blandford) and Mr. A. J. Payne (Homerton).

As for consolation prizes, Miss F. M. Overton (Upper Tooting), Mr. R. M. Munro (Nantwich), Major W. E. W. Howard (Marino, Ireland) have the strongest claims; Mr. E. Handscomb (West Norwood) also accused Miss Pettigrew and provided an answer to C, though he went astray in A and B.

A. C. Cawker (S. E. 27) had his eye on Miss Pettigrew; but, reluctant (unlike some others) to "invent" his own evidence, he decided properly enough that at the end of the fifth instalment "motive so far is lacking." Finally, I consider that Felix Fereday (Upper Tooting) deserves a consolation prize: it is true that he plumped for Robert Ellis and Mrs. Hulk, but in my opinion he went more thoroughly than any other competitor into the "questionable" aspects of the evidence before the listener. If a seventh consolation prize is to be offered I should myself award it, quite illogically, to J. E. F. Coningham (Tonbridge) on the strength of one comment: "The good Inspector seemed to attach some importance to the fact that Mrs. Hulk was slicing beef late. Why ever shouldn't she?"

MILWARD KENNEDY

APPENDIX II

*The following letter and editor's reply appeared
in* The Listener, *February 11, 1931*

Is your serial detective story, "The Scoop,"
planned as a whole by a committee of all the authors before the publication (or broadcasting) of
chapter one? If the outline of the plot is settled
in this way (as seems reasonable) what latitude
is each author allowed in the section for which
he is personally responsible? If the story is not
planned beforehand, or the outline of the plot
definitely settled by writer No. 1, does each author merely keep the ball rolling by exploiting his
or her own vein of fiction, trusting to the last
member of the team to wind up the proceedings
as he thinks best?

I have not seen any explanation in print of the
constructional method employed in this or in the
previous serial of a similar type. If the plot is a
matter of chance, the story has little to recom-
mend it. A complete production by any one writer

would come nearer to Father Knox's standard for good detective fiction.

Manchester   J.R.D.

A correspondent, whose letter we publish elsewhere, expresses curiosity concerning the method employed in planning broadcast detective serials like "Behind the Screen" and "The Scoop." Miss Dorothy Sayers has had a hand in both enterprises, and has been the organising genius behind "The Scoop," coordinating the different contributions as well as making her own. We have pressed her to reveal the secrets of her detective workshop in this case, and here is her reply: "The plot of 'The Scoop' was planned in rough outline by all the authors in committee before the broadcasting of Chapter I. After this, each writer worked to a sketch-outline of what his instalment was to contain, any point of detail which arose in the course of working the chapter out being decided in consultation with myself and his other fellow-authors. As regards the actual writing, each author was left free to develop his own style and method. Generally speaking, whoever introduces a new character is responsible for laying down that character's general appearance, method of speech, etc., and other writers are, of course, expected to carry it along on the same lines. In 'Behind the Screen' a somewhat different method was employed. In this, the first three authors carried the story along according to their own several fancies; while the last three used their wits, in consultation, to unravel the clues presented to them by the first three. There is no reason why a perfectly 'correct' detective story should not be produced, even where the plot is not planned in collaboration at all. If each writer writes with a definite solution in mind and lays his clues properly, those clues can be picked up and worked to a satisfactory conclusion by a subsequent writer." The proof of a pudding is in the eating, and we may add to Miss Sayers' last words the information that a book on these lines is actually being written by members of the Detection Club, for publication this year.